Reddy

by

J L Wilson

Reddy

Cover Art by *The Wild Rose Press, Inc.*

The Wild Rose Press, Inc.
PO Box 708
Adams Basin, NY 14410-0708
Visit us at www.thewildrosepress.com

Publishing History
First Edition, 2025
Trade Paperback ISBN 978-1-5092-6187-1
Digital ISBN 978-1-5092-6188-8

Published in the United States of America

Chapter 1

October 1, five years ago
"Reddy, while it's a pity your marriage didn't work out, at least you got something out of it. Two hundred thousand dollars is nothing to sneeze at." My grandmother turned from the passenger seat to regard me, her sharp green eyes assessing my current level of despair.

I glared at her from my spot on the back seat of the MomMobile, my mother's spacious sedan. "Don't call me Reddy," I snapped. "I told you. I prefer Rebeka."

My mother shot me an admonishing glance in the rear-view mirror. "Rebeka Evelyn Danforth. Don't use that tone of voice with your elders."

Thank you, Mother. Sure enough, that crack about 'elders' got my grandma going.

"Who are you calling elderly?" My grandmother, Rose Elizabeth Davis, a.k.a Reddy One, glared at my mother. "I'm eighty-five years old. I'm not in my dotage."

"Yet," I muttered.

"Don't add fuel to the fire." My mother, Ruth Ellen Duffy, always placid, always calm, smiled serenely. "I admit, it was a disappointment that your marriage didn't last."

"Asshole ran off with a girl half his age," Grandmother mumbled. "Good riddance. Reddy

1

deserves every penny she got. She helped build that company as much as Asshole did. It's because of her they were able to expand."

"Thank you," I said to the old woman.

"However." My mother, a.k.a. Reddy Two, raised her voice. "It gives you a nice nest egg to begin planning for your future. I think we'll diversify and invest more heavily in Google. I heard they have a new phone coming out."

"Who needs a mobile phone?" Grandmother pointed to a pay phone outside Wiley's Drug Store on the corner of Woodland and Lake. "There are phones everywhere."

"Not anymore. I think that's the last one in town."

Grandmother snorted. "Don't know why people need to talk to each other all the time."

"They don't talk. They text. Or play games or watch movies."

"That reminds me. Netflix. I think we'll consider some of the other streaming services. In addition, I think we'll buy stock in virtual reality companies." Mother nodded thoughtfully.

"Sure. Fine." I knew nothing about investing but my mother was a whiz. She had learned from my late father who had an uncanny ability to find the next Big Thing to invest in. She'd already doubled my retirement fund by investing in Apple and Google years earlier.

I planned to hand over the cash settlement and let her work her magic. I wanted to put my whole fiasco of a marriage behind me where it belonged. I was still smarting from a prolonged haggle over the company my ex-husband, Doug, and I built.

Visit the Wild was an expedition-experience company that we started. We specialized in comfortable into-the-woods camping trips, with city folk staying at cabins in the north woods of Minnesota where we were based. In the winter we hosted some dog sled adventures. In the summer it was canoeing and hiking. We began small here in Perrault, Minnesota and expanded to Duluth after ten years of successful operation.

Doug handled the Duluth store and that's where he met his next soulmate, twenty-five-year-old Julie, slim, svelte, and outdoorsy. At the age of forty-four, I was relegated to Ancient Status while he cheerfully embarked on a new life with a new wife. Our ten-year marriage was left in the dust.

I got the original business, a lump sum, and our small house in Perrault, a town proudly North of Nowhere on the edge of the Boundary Waters in northern Minnesota. There was one major road in and out. It often closed in the winter due to blizzards and in the summer due to bears or moose wandering the area.

I was currently riding with my mother and grandmother to pick out new furniture for my home. Reddy One and Reddy Two had swept into my little bungalow, grabbed me, and dragged me to the MomMobile.

"We are throwing out your old life and getting you a new one," my mother declared. We were on our way to Eveleth, the nearest town of any size, to survey the offerings in the two furniture stores.

I was secretly glad they grabbed me. I had been moping around the house for the past three weeks since the divorce was finalized. I needed a kick in the pants to get my world moving again.

"Be careful at that intersection," I cautioned, eyeing the speedometer which was creeping up to sixty. "They put in a stop sign there last week."

"What a stupid waste of taxpayer dollars. We're on a highway. Who puts a stop sign on a highway?" Grandmother fumbled for the visor. "I hate when the sun gets so low in the sky. Seems like you can never get away from it."

"At least it's a bright sunny day. Pretty soon we'll be complaining about wind chill and snow." Mother hummed softly as she tapped the steering wheel. I recognized "Hello Goodbye." She'd been revisiting the Beatles lately. "Let's go to JC Penney first then we can go to Akron's."

"We should shop local first then go to one of the national chains." Grandmother leaned forward. "Those trees are pretty, aren't they? I always say autumn is our reward for hanging around and enduring winter instead of fleeing to Florida like some wussies I know."

Mother let up on the gas when we topped a hill. I glimpsed the intersection ahead where a smaller highway came in from the right and a county road came in from the left. Tall pine and cedar trees lined the roads, casting shadows on the pavement.

"It's less expensive at JCP," Mother said placidly.

"She has money to spend."

"Rebeka needs to be careful with her finances. If we invest it right, she'll only have to work part-time and only then because of the health care benefits. I swear, I don't know what the country is coming to. It costs so much these days for—"

"Watch out," I warned. "The intersection is right ahead."

"Quit being a back seat driver." Grandmother turned to slap my leg.

The road on the right held a logging truck, slowing for the intersection. When we neared the stop sign a small blue sedan shot out of the woods on our left, from the county road. It was on my side of the car, so I had a good view inside.

A man was driving, a woman in the front seat next to him. It appeared that someone else was wedged in between them. A kid? That's not right. The kid should be in a car seat or at least in the back seat.

The man was gesturing angrily, arms waving.

Wait a minute. Arms? Both arms? Didn't he have a hand on the wheel?

It happened so fast. The blue sedan aimed for us like a torpedo guided to a ship. I had time for a yell—"There's a car!"

Then we were hit. The sedan rammed our car between the front and the back seats on the driver's side. Stupid me, I wasn't wearing a seat belt. I was thrown hard against the passenger side of the car, my head hitting the window.

The world went black.

****

October 1, today

I held on to Grandmother's arm, helping her out of my SUV. She was still somewhat mobile, but she was ninety and the ground around Mother's grave was uneven.

We had been making these yearly visits for the past three years. The accident five years earlier left me in a coma for almost a month with a concussion and a broken hip, leg, and arm. Grandmother escaped with a fractured arm and severe bruising.

Mother took the brunt of the hit with broken legs,

arm, and hip. While the injuries contributed to her ill health it was the attendant legal wranglings that I think ruined her. Mother had previously had an unshakeable trust in humanity, but the accident destroyed that. She didn't fully recover and died of a heart attack two years after the crash, a week after the anniversary of the accident.

Grandmother and I both blamed the accident for my mother's death. We made this pilgrimage every October, this time on a Saturday. It was a beautiful fall day. The Perrault cemetery had an abundance of trees and not the evergreens so common in this part of northern Minnesota. Birch, maple, and oaks were scattered here and there, many in gorgeous fall color.

"I don't know how many more years I can do this." Grandmother stabbed her cane into the turf, softened by rain the day before.

She said the same thing every year, so I didn't worry too much about some kind of prophecy on her part coming true. "I'm glad to have you with me. I miss her."

"She was taken before her time, thanks to that no-good Boyd Wulfson," Grandmother muttered. "People like that shouldn't be allowed to walk the earth, not after what he did."

I agreed with her, but I kept my opinion to myself. Life isn't fair and sometimes bad shit happens to good people. "Well, he did have to pay a price. His wife died, his child was put into foster care, he paid a fine, and he went to prison for four years."

"A pittance compared to the damage he did. It was his third conviction for reckless driving. Third!" Grandmother jerked her cane, upending the flowers in the plastic holder pushed into the ground.

I used that as an opportunity to get rid of the old blooms and put in the fresh flowers I brought while Grandmother continued her rant. "It was the middle of the day, and he was drinking. Who drinks that much in the middle of the day? And where did he even get the money to drink? He was jobless." She shook her head, white hair waving in the gentle breeze. "Worthless trash."

"His wife worked," I murmured. "Perhaps she gave him the money. Let's face it, maybe she wanted him out of the house."

"Living out there in the woods, off the grid with no electric and no heat. Fireplace, wood stove, and solar panels. Damn hippies." She was working up a good head of steam. I'd heard it all before, of course. "Preppers." She injected a wealth of disgust into the word. "A bunch of crazy idiots who think the sky is falling and hiding out in a bunker will save their sorry asses."

Heaven knows, Perrault attracted all kinds of people because we were so far removed from 'civilization'. We had our share of back-to-nature hippies, commune enthusiasts, and supposed woodsmen who loved to channel their inner Daniel Boone. Few of them stuck around after the first winter. The ones who did kept to themselves and thankfully seldom crossed paths with anyone from town.

Except when they got drunk and rammed into another car.

"They should have removed that child from their custody long before they did. Lord knows what kind of damage was done to that impressionable mind." Grandmother leaned over carefully and rested her hand on Mother's tombstone.

Ruth Elizabeth Duffy. Beloved wife, mother, daughter. It was next to my father's, with a similar inscription. *Charles Duffy. Beloved husband, father, son.* Those simple words truly did sum up their lives. My father died when I was ten years old and my mother had to become the breadwinner, a task she took up with great enthusiasm and success. She never loved anyone else. I don't think she even considered the idea. My father had been the one love of her life.

I slipped my arm through my grandmother's. Odd that such marital happiness came to my mother but eluded my grandmother and me. It was as though the Happy Fairy tapped one generation and skipped the others.

I never knew my grandfather. He abandoned his family after my mother was born and was never heard from since. My grandmother divorced him *in absentia* and had a succession of 'gentlemen friends' over the years, but she refused to remarry.

"I will never allow another man to take control of my heart," she declared more than once.

I could sympathize since the only man I had given my heart to had rejected it. Although, to be honest, Doug and I weren't soulmates, not the way my parents were. In the five years since my divorce, I had come to realize that I was better off without him.

"Thank you, Reddy Two." I touched Mother's stone, blessing her for the foresight to invest my money properly. Because of her investments and my inheritance, I was comfortably situated as long as I was somewhat frugal. That suited me. I had no extravagant habits and nothing in particular I needed to fritter my money on.

"You never liked that nickname." Grandmother shot me a surprised look, one eyebrow crooked up in question.

"It was a quirk of fate that we have the same initials." I leaned slightly against her, more of a nudge than a lean. "I was always Red in school because of my hair. I guess I was hoping once I graduated, I would get away from it."

"You got that beautiful titian hair and white skin from your father. He was such a handsome man. And your mother—well, she was the prettiest girl in town." Grandmother smiled fondly at the tombstone. "You take after your parents. So beautiful."

I laughed softly. "You're no slouch yourself." I wasn't lying. She was a stately, beautiful old lady, tall and only slightly stooped with abundant white hair that was expertly coiffed in a confection of curls and swirls. She reminded me of a tall and slender Betty White both in appearance and personality. Perky with a bite, pretty without being pretentious.

"I like your hair that way." Grandmother eyed my new hairdo, short at the nape but longer on the top and sides. I had natural waves, giving my hair good bounce, plus it was thick as well. With a few spritzes from a water bottle I could get it to behave, pushed back from my face or held back with a headband or barrette.

"I think I finally found my style. It's only taken me fifty years."

"I'm glad you grew out of the hair-down-to-your-waist phase. You were like a popsicle stick with that red hair and your skinny legs."

I laughed at the image. I was slender, another thing to thank my mother and father for. "Good genes from the

9

people in the family. I'm not sure about my father's family, though. I may have a skeleton or two in that closet." My father had been an orphan, raised in foster care. No one had any idea who his parents were.

"I doubt it." She sighed. "A person shouldn't outlive their children. It makes me feel old."

"I miss her. I still find myself thinking, 'oh, I'll call Mother and tell her about that' and then I remember." I sighed as well. "I'm reminded of that stupid accident whenever the weather changes and my new hip goes crazy."

Grandmother rubbed her arm. "I know what you mean." We stood for another moment then she said "Well, I suppose we'd better wrap this up so I can get back to the CF."

She delighted in using that abbreviation for her care facility, knowing full well that it also meant something completely different in urban slang. Grandmother had a one-bedroom assisted living apartment in a facility nestled right in the middle of town, straddling The Border. That was the name that residents used for Wolf Way, the road that divided the old part of town on the west from the new part of town on the east. My store was a few blocks away from her care facility in the old part of town.

"Can I dine with you?" I asked.

"Of course. And I have a nice bottle of white wine that will go nicely with our meal. I believe it's chicken tetrazzini today or something that passes for that. Perhaps we should drink the wine before we go to the dining room." She clung to my arm when we began our laborious progress back to the car.

"If we drink the wine before we walk to the dining

room, we might not make it to the dining room."

"True. Tell you what. Let's go through a drive-through and get some burgers and take them to the park and have a picnic. Your mother loved burgers." She squinted at the sun. "It isn't five yet. We still have time before the sun goes down."

"What about the wine?"

"We'll buy some at the liquor store on our way and I'll save my bottle for another day." She nudged me. "What do you say? Do you need to go to work today? Busy season's wrapping up, isn't it?"

"Yep. Only a few fishermen out and about and it's too early for the snowmobilers. We've gone to winter hours on the weekend, so we closed early. A picnic sounds good. You talked me into it."

We got to the SUV, and I started to tuck her in. Grandmother grasped the door, peering over the top of the car. "Who's that? He's like that actor from NCIS, that Harmon guy."

I followed her gaze and saw a man standing a few tombstone rows away, watching us. Even from a distance I could see how blue his eyes were. It was startling. His thick silver hair was brushed back from his face. He wore a tweedy grey sports coat over a dark sweater with black jeans.

There was something in the way he stood that made me wonder if he was in the military. Then I shook my head. NCIS, of course. The power of suggestion.

"I don't know who it is. Perrault does have over 8000 people. I don't know everybody." I returned to the task of getting her safely into the car, holding her arm and helping her lower herself carefully.

"Good-looking men don't live in Perrault. He must

be an outsider." Grandmother settled back on the seat with a contented sigh. "I'm glad you have an SUV. It's easier to get in and out of than Woody's old Buick."

Woody, a.k.a. Woodrow Wilson Hunter, was Grandmother's 'suitor', so called because, as she said, he suited her. He lived three doors away from her in the CF.

"After our accident, I wanted to drive a tank. This is as close as I could get to it and still be able to afford it." I patted the roof of my trusty Subaru, which I had named Stu. "Drive-through and picnic, coming up." I closed the door and walked around the car.

The man was still there, hands in his pants pockets. I didn't know the layout of the cemetery well, so I wasn't sure who was buried in that section. From the way he stood I don't think he was there to pay his respects. Well, it was not my problem if someone wanted to wander around the gravestones on a pristine October afternoon.

I slid behind the wheel, and we drove north into town. "I'm surprised Woody is still driving. I thought he was going to sell the Buick to his grandson."

"We only go around town. We never go out on the highway much as we might like to get out of town now and again and go to the city."

We? Good heavens, Grandmother was ninety and Woody was two years younger. They had no business being on the road much less contemplating a drive on the highway to 'the city', which was Duluth.

"We all get the urge to see new places occasionally," I agreed.

"And you can pick up and do so if you want to." She tapped her cane on the floor. "I'm not complaining. You're a sweetheart to come over as much as you do. It's just that, well, when a person gets older, you lose your independence."

Grandmother stared wistfully out her window, her profile that of a woman twenty years younger than her age. Great bones and skin care. I hoped I inherited her genes.

"I know. It must be frustrating. Let's plan a trip to the Twin Cities before the snow sets in. We'll go to the Guthrie and take in a play. We'll get good seats with your handicapped status. Maybe we can go the Galleria Mall and see how the rich folk spend their money. I'll rent one of those wheelchair things and you can zip around the halls."

She snorted with laughter. "Be careful, Minneapolis, here come the Reddy girls."

I checked the rear-view mirror and saw a car behind us, a small SUV. Was that man following us? This wasn't a well-traveled road but there were other streets branching off it. And heaven knows SUVs were common in this part of the world where snow often got as high as my waist and all-wheel drive was a necessity, not a social statement.

We got to the Flip Shack which was conveniently located next to Bob's Booze Boutique on the old side of town. I left Grandmother at Bob's to select our vintage, and I went to the Shack to get our lunches. I had a pleasant chat with the teenager manning the counter, a young girl who was a fishing guide for us in the summer months. When I emerged, I found Grandmother waiting by the car, one of BBB's clerks with her.

"He was afraid I'd drop the bottle, so he carried out for me," she explained. We got in the car again, bottle of wine and food on the back seat then we headed for the park adjacent to the CF.

"I'll text Woody and he can join us," she said. "I'll split my burger with him."

"You should have told me. I would have gotten a burger for him, too."

"At my age I can't eat a full meal anyway. I'm happy to share. I had the boys at the liquor store set me up with silverware and cups so we're good to go." She flourished some plasticware and paper cups. "I told them we were picnicking, and they tossed 'em in with the wine. I'd better get hold of Woody. It takes him a while to get going."

Grandmother dug in her handbag and pulled out a smartphone. I sneaked covert glances at her as she laboriously typed a message, one letter at a time. We were almost at the park by the time she finished.

"I can't get the hang of that thumb typing," she said, tucking the phone back in the bag. "I tried and ended up typing gibberish."

"I think you're pretty awesome to do any typing, and on a smart phone no less," I assured her. We parked near one of the picnic bench areas in the sun where I got her and the lunch fare seated. Grandmother fastidiously sliced her burger in half while I dug in.

I was wiping the juice from my first few bites of the Flip Shack Special when I spied Woody tootling over from the CF in his bright red golf cart. He swung onto the sidewalk, chugging along until he got to the park road, then he hung a sharp left and shot toward us.

"He does love to drive his cart," Grandmother said placidly while the old man bore down on us. "He misses driving a squad car."

"All he needs are lights and sirens and he'd be able to chase criminals. He doesn't observe any speed limits, does he?" I grinned at the sight of Woody, small and compact, his white hair partially hidden by a Twins baseball cap squashed on his head, the bill backward. His bright purple Minnesota Vikings sweatshirt was like a beacon in the sunlight.

He waved wildly while he approached. "Thanks for the invite, girls!" he shouted. "I was afraid I'd be stuck at dinner with Crazy Betty."

Betty was another CF resident who had her eye on Woody. She did all she could to spend time with him, hanging around when he attended group activities, changing the place holders at lunch so she could sit at his table, and planning her visits to the mailboxes when he made his visits.

"I swear, Betty is going to hogtie him sometime and haul him away. I don't know what she'd do if she got him. At our age, all we do is fall asleep in front of television together." Grandmother waved a French fry in reply to his shout, sprinkling ketchup drops on the table.

Woody pulled to a stop next to the table and got out. I kept an eye on him as he moved. He'd been wounded years earlier and his left leg now and again gave way. He had his cane today and leaned heavily on it, so I knew it was bothering him. He sank on the bench next to Grandmother and beamed at me.

Woody reminded me of a somewhat slender Santa with his round face, twinkling eyes, and stocky body. He'd been the Chief of Police for years until he retired. Then he took a job as a consulting deputy, helping out now and again until he finally retired at the age of eighty. But I know that he still dropped in at the station occasionally to shoot the breeze with 'the boys'.

"It's such a pretty day. Makes sense to spend it

outside here instead of in there with the old folks." He grinned at me then nudged Grandmother, whose eyes twinkled fondly at him.

"Might be one of the last good weeks until the snow flies. We need to take advantage of it." Grandmother pushed her burger toward him while I poured him a glass of wine. "Eat up, Chief."

"You know how to treat me right, Rosie." He toasted me with the wine. "I wonder if it's legal to be drinking like this out in public. If we're not careful, Chief Jake Grimly might show up and give us a talking to." He winked at me as he said it.

"It was one date," I protested. "One date." Would I never live this down?

"I don't know. Seems to me he's been carrying the torch for you. Kind of like Crazy Betty. Every time you turn around, there he is."

I didn't want to admit it, but he was right. I'd known Jake most of my life since we both grew up in Perrault. We both left for college and came back at different times, me to marry Doug and start a business and Jake returning six years ago to take the Chief of Police job. He had married and divorced while away from Perrault, so he was an eligible bachelor. Jake was a big help to us after the accident during the legal wranglings.

"Well, that takes some nerve," Grandmother stated.

"What does?"

"There he is. That man again." She stared over my shoulder at the entry to the park.

"What?" I swiveled on the picnic bench. She was right. An SUV was pulling into the parking area. It appeared to be the same man behind the wheel and the same SUV that had followed us from the cemetery. "Are we being stalked?"

"Not we, dear. You." Grandmother beamed at me. "What would he want with an old lady like me? Let's see what this is about. It's rather exciting, a strange man follows you around town and accosts you in public. I wonder why."

"I'll find out why." Woody laboriously managed to extricate himself from the picnic bench, swinging his legs out preparatory to standing. "You girls stay here. I'll handle this."

Oh, Lord. I had visions of elderly mayhem dancing in my head. "Woody, no, that's okay. I'll talk to him."

"No, you let me see what this guy wants. I've dealt with his kind before." He hitched up his sagging blue jeans, grabbed his cane, and set off to face the SUV, which had pulled into a parking slot not far away.

Grandmother dabbed her mouth with a paper napkin. "I think you should go with him, dear. I know he has the knowledge to cope with a situation like this, but I'm not sure he has the physical wherewithal anymore."

I grabbed a fry and stood. "Hang on. It's probably somebody who's lost who wants directions."

"I doubt that, dear. I think he's a man who has a goal in mind and unless I'm mistaken, his goal is you." She smiled brightly. "What a nice surprise."

"I don't need surprises," I muttered, hurrying after Woody. He had a head start on me, but I was able to catch up to him as the man exited his car, standing beside it and watching us approach. "Woody, hang on."

"You can back me up, but you let me do the talking, Reddy. I may be old, but I still remember how to deal with men like him." He strode up to the man, his face set and harsh.

That was his cop face, I realized. "Okay, well, don't hurt him."

He winked. "I'll restrain myself." He came to a stop. "Who are you, sir, and why are you following these ladies?"

"Who are you and why do you think I'm following them?" The man spoke in a polite, low voice, his blue-eyed gaze shifting from me to Woody then back to me. Up close I could see he did resemble the actor except his hair was much thicker and had a wave in its grey-black depths. His nose was also a bit off-center.

Maybe broken once, I decided. I'd seen enough canoeing accidents to recognize what it was.

"I am a friend of these women. I've lived in this town all my life and I believe you're a stranger. Please identify yourself." Woody placed both hands on his cane, his fingers flexing on the top which was carved in the shape of a wolf's head.

"I don't have to identify myself to you or anyone else." There was a definite note of defiance in the stranger's even, calm voice.

"Now see here. You cannot go around following people." Woody moved forward.

I stepped between them. "Woody, it's okay. I'll handle this." I turned to the stranger. "Excuse me, but I don't believe—"

"Let me handle it, Reddy." Woody tried to push past me, but I got tangled up with his cane. I lost my balance and teetered precariously then tipped over, falling into the stranger, who managed to catch me. I stared up into his bright blue eyes.

He appeared as surprised as I felt. I tried to extricate myself, but he had me in a grip. I struggled and he still didn't release me.

To my shock, he pulled me closer and leaned over to whisper in my ear. I shivered at the feeling of his warm breath.

"Mrs. Danforth, we need to talk. I need your help to find a killer."

Chapter 2

I peered owlishly at him. His eyes were a pale blue surrounded by a line of dark blue. It made his gaze piercing, an adjective I'd heard before but had never experienced firsthand. "What did you say?"

He helped me right myself, subtly moving me with him so we had more distance between us and Woody. "We need to talk in private."

"Bullshit," Woody declared. "I am friends with Reddy's family. Anything you want to say to her, you say in my hearing." He waved wildly behind him. "And her grandmother's."

I looked back at Grandmother. Damn, she was starting to slide along the picnic bench. She'd try to join us if I didn't nip it in the bud.

"I don't know what you want, but my dinner is getting cold," I said. "You can speak to me while I eat. Anything you have to say you can say in front of Mr. Hunter and my grandmother."

Woody regarded the man with undisguised suspicion. "You don't even know Reddy and you want to talk to her in private? That doesn't sound right."

The man stiffened. I shifted position when I felt him still holding my arm. I jerked it, and he let me go. I narrowly avoided bumping into Woody, who was standing next to me.

"I know it sounds odd, but I need to talk to Mrs.

Danforth," he said. "And her grandmother. They both might be in danger."

Woody glared at him for a long second then he nodded abruptly. "You can talk to them, but I want to be there. I don't want you left alone with them. I have 911 on speed dial on my phone and I know the boys at the station. If I give a holler your ass will be tossed in the slammer so fast you won't know what happened. So don't try anything. Come on, Reddy."

He took my arm and began shuffling back to Grandmother, who was now standing by the picnic table, one hand flat on its surface.

"You wait for us, Grandmother," I warned while we walked to her. "Don't you dare move without me."

She waved with her free hand, which held a French fry. "Good thing you're coming over here. I was getting ready to call the police." To my relief she sat on the bench, moving over to make room for Woody when we got to her.

The stranger hesitated then went to the far end of the table, standing where he could see each of us. I resumed my seat and took another bite of my burger, eyeing him warily.

"I know this must appear odd, Mrs. Danforth, but I needed to talk to you, and it seemed best to approach you in person." The man reached for his back pocket as though going for his wallet. Then he frowned and shook his head.

"Ms.," I corrected. "I'm no longer married."

"Thank God," Grandmother muttered. "Danforth was an asshole. He didn't deserve you. Which wife is he on now? Three? Four?"

I sighed. "Doug searches for love in all the wrong

places. That's all."

"He's not searching for love. He's searching for the fountain of youth. You were his second fountain of youth and when he drained you he moved on." She frowned at the stranger. "Her ex keeps marrying younger and younger women. Someday he'll run out of stupid girls who think he's a meal ticket."

I didn't dare tell her that Doug had contacted me the past week. He and I had been in touch occasionally through the years because of store business. Both operated completely independently but there was some overlap.

But this wasn't about the store, no, Doug was contrite that his newest ex-wife, the lovely Julie, the one he left me for, had set up shop in Perrault in direct competition to me. Her store, Dip Your Oar, was on the new side of town on the east, while mine was on the old side of town on the west.

Doug had apologized profusely for Julie's 'betrayal' as he called it. He had apparently spoken often about Perrault and its unique position as a gateway to the wilderness, a gateway that had only one or two high-end outfitters. He mentioned in passing that he'd told Julie how he had urged me to upgrade our Perrault store but been overruled.

That was bullshit, of course. Doug had an extremely selective memory. The few times I had ordered more expensive gear he'd whined and moaned. I suppose that's what gave Julie the idea to open her 'adventure boutique' stocked with expensive clothing and equipment, more suited to an Aspen or Vail outing than a one-week stay in the North Woods. I had successfully managed to avoid her in the three months since she opened her venture in a storefront on Main Street.

Doug also seemed anxious about his upcoming nuptials to Wife Number Three, someone named Susan he met in the Twin Cities. Doug was now in his mid-fifties and Wife Number Three was twenty. But I suspected he wasn't after relationship advice.

What he wanted was help with the Duluth store, which had suffered under his and Julie's guidance. Good Lord, I'd never hear the end of it if I told Grandmother that he'd been in touch. It was bad enough that Julie was here, and Grandmother had caught wind of that. It took a lot of persuading on my part to prevent her from storming the storefront and running Julie out of town.

"Grandmother, please. I'm sure the gentleman isn't interested in the history of my last name." The man did appear bemused. Or maybe confused. "How can I help you, Mr. ..." I eyed him expectantly.

"I'm Detective—" He stopped and frowned again. "Sorry. I just retired. I'm used to showing my credentials and—Anyway, my name is G.C. Jager. I want to talk with you about the accident five years ago."

"Detective?" Grandmother perked up at this. "From where? Duluth? That's where the asshole lives. What did he do?"

"Grandmother, please. Let the man talk."

"I was on the San Francisco PD for most of my career." The man didn't seem happy that he was no longer there. In fact, he seemed downright peeved. I suppose Perrault, Minnesota was quite a change from the city by the Bay. At least he had dressed for autumn. His jacket appeared warm, and the sweater was heavy and thick.

"Why are you here in our little corner of God's

paradise?" Grandmother waved expansively, French fry in hand.

Woody plucked it from her grasp with a grin. "Thank you, Reddy One."

"Reddy?" The stranger's eyebrows drew together when he frowned at me. "Isn't that your name? That's what he called you."

"I'm Reddy One. My daughter was Reddy Two. And Rebeka is Reddy Three. Most folks call me Rosie anymore, so Rebeka inherited the title." Grandmother watched him, her green eyes alert and calculating. "Why are you here and why do you need to talk to my granddaughter?"

"It's a long and somewhat complicated story." He gestured to the picnic bench. "Would you mind if I sat while I tell it? I had an injury. It acts up sometimes." Again, he appeared peeved at having to admit he may have a frailty.

I jerked a thumb at the end of my bench, almost losing my grip on the burger to do so. I noticed his left leg didn't move as easily as his right. Woody's eyes were on the stranger, and I think he saw, too. There wasn't much that escaped that old cop's notice.

"Why are you so far from home, Mr. Jager?" I asked politely.

He clasped his hands on the picnic top. His hands were large, and he didn't wear any rings. "About twenty years ago, I was married to a great woman. Candace Lupin. She had a daughter, Mindy, from a former marriage as well as a son, Jason. Mindy was fourteen and Jason was sixteen." Jager smiled briefly when he mentioned their names. "Our marriage didn't work out. Candy couldn't handle being a detective's wife. It's pretty stressful and I was involved in some high profile, ugly cases."

He took a deep breath. "We got divorced when Mindy was twenty-one. I stayed close with the family, even when Candy remarried, and they moved to Minnesota where her new husband got a job in St. Paul."

Third time's the charm for the ex? Jager didn't appear too cut up about his ex-wife remarrying, so maybe he was fine with it.

"Fast forward a few years. Six years ago, Mindy was in a boating accident, and she needed a blood transfusion. She developed a transfusion reaction that damaged her kidneys."

"Wow. You don't hear much about that kind of thing," Grandmother noted.

"It's rare but it happens. She went on dialysis and was put on a donor waiting list. This is where your accident comes into the picture. Mrs. Wulfson, the wife of the man who hit you in that accident, was an organ donor. She had registered with the state. Tests were run and she was a good match for Mindy. They did a kidney transplant and Mindy recovered nicely. No transplant reaction, no rejection. Her doctors gave her a clean bill of health."

"At the time of the accident, I didn't know Wulfson was a donor," I said. "Of course, I found out about it later." I scowled at the remains of my burger, pushing it away as though it was responsible for my annoyance.

Jager shot me a confused look but continued when I didn't offer an explanation. "Two years ago, Mindy died. She had just gotten married. She and her husband were living in St. Louis. It was sudden. A heart attack."

"Heart attack?" Grandmother asked. "How old was

she?"

"Thirty-two." Jager blew out a sigh. "She was alone at home. Her husband came home and found her."

"Like Mother," I murmured. "How do we fit in?" I gestured to Grandmother, sitting across from me.

"I'm trying to figure out what might have gone wrong. I decided that I'd talk to Mr. Wulfson. If you could tell me about the accident, I'd know how to talk to him."

"Don't try," Grandmother advised. "He's batshit crazy."

Jager straightened in surprise. "Why do you say that?"

"Because he sued us for wrongful death," Grandmother spat. "He tried to claim that my daughter, Ruth, was at fault. Bullshit, of course. We had a witness to the whole thing. Wulfson ran the stop sign and there was nothing Ruth could do to avoid him."

"Could you—would you tell me what happened?" Jager stared uncertainly from me to Grandmother. "I'm sorry if it's a painful memory. But I need to understand what happened so I can approach Wulfson and maybe get answers. Candy and I may be divorced but we're still friends and the kids were a big part of my life. They still are."

He appeared so disconsolate that I took pity on him. "We were driving south on Highway 1, on our way to Eveleth," I said. "That's the main road going in and out of town. There are secondary, side roads, but the highway is the fastest way to get anywhere. Mother was driving. It was this time of year. The sun is so low in the sky that it gets hard to see things sometimes. The highway department had put in a new interchange where the logging road meets the highway, with a smaller county road off to one side."

I arranged a few French fries on the picnic top to show him what I meant.

"We were coming over the hill, here." Grandmother tapped the Highway 1 French fry. "Ruthie was going the speed limit, and she knew a new intersection was ahead. That bastard Boyd Wulfson came out of nowhere and hit us."

"As Grandmother said," and I shot her a quelling glance, "we were slowing for the stop sign. A logging truck came from the road on the right." I tapped that French fry. "It had stopped at the intersection. We were slowing when Wulfson's car came from the left and hit us in the side. It crushed the driver side of the car, pushed us off the road, and we spun into the ditch."

I still had nightmares about that accident, remembering the sickening, out-of-control feeling when the car did that whirling screech across the pavement.

"That wasn't the worst of it." Grandmother swept the French fries off the table, her voice trembling with outrage.

"Calm down, Rosie." Woody put his hand on hers, his gnarled, arthritic fingers stroking over the fine bones of her fingers. "Let Reddy tell it. You relax."

Grandmother shot him a glare but gave an abrupt nod. "Tell him, Reddy."

"It's hard to believe anything would be worse than such a terrible accident," Jager said sympathetically.

"Mother and I took the brunt of the hit. I had a bad concussion, and I was kept sedated for weeks while my body healed. Fractured ribs and arm, broken leg and hip. Mother had two broken legs, a broken hip and arm. We both had massive bruising and that complicated our recovery. We were hospitalized off and on for months. While we were in the hospital, Wulfson sued us. He claimed we were responsible for his wife's death."

"Asshole," Grandmother muttered darkly. "Crazy bastard."

"He didn't know that his wife had signed up to be an organ donor," Woody said, raising his voice to override Grandmother. "He claimed that the accident was tantamount to murder. It was a ploy for him to get out of it. He had a record of drunk driving, and he was impaired. Not bad but bad enough."

"Middle of the day." Grandmother pounded the table with her free hand, the other one still imprisoned by Woody.

"We had several nasty months with the insurance companies, wrangling over who was at fault. When the driver of the logging truck testified that Wulfson had run the stop sign, Wulfson tried to kill the man. He overturned the table in the courtroom and lunged for the logger. He wanted to strangle the man."

"Batshit crazy," Grandmother declared.

"It dragged on for over a year. He was doing everything he could to avoid prison. He sued us on behalf of his child, who had been in the car at the time. He claimed the accident caused her permanent trauma and when his custody of the child was taken away from him, he came after me."

I shot a warning glare at Grandmother, who appeared ready to leap to her feet and start yelling. "He physically attacked me at my store, shoved me into a rack of clothing and hit me with his fists." Now my voice trembled at the memory.

"That was it," Woody said with satisfaction. "You don't go around beating up on people because you think they're in the wrong. He caused the accident, and he refused to accept any responsibility for it. The judge threw the book at him. He got six years in prison because it wasn't his first offense. His daughter was handed over to foster care. That was ugly." Woody shook his head.

"What do you mean?" Jager sounded both shocked and sympathetic. I appreciated it. It was still so easy to remember how it felt to be so helpless, to be constantly peering over my shoulder for that madman.

"A hearing was held to determine custody of the child. Wulfson had been sentenced to prison, but he refused to cede parental rights. He insisted his daughter remain at their house alone. Hell, she was only thirteen or so at the time. He said if she went into foster care, he'd never see her again. They had a shouting, screaming scene at the court hearing. The boys at the station told me about it."

Jager nodded his understanding. Of course, he was an ex-cop. He probably understood the Cop Guy Network.

"Wulfson and Louise, the girl, were yelling about how the government was infringing on their freedoms and how they'd make sure nobody could take their property. The girl had to be physically restrained and gagged. Lord, she was a foul-mouthed little thing. She was an itty-bitty kid, but she fought like a berserker." Woody shook his head mournfully, white hair wisping in the breeze. "She did go into foster care, and I heard she was adopted."

"I'm sorry to rake up old wounds," Jager said. "It sounds like he was certifiable."

"I wish he was. Maybe he'd still be locked up." I bundled up my food wrappers and jammed them back into the paper sack they came in.

"He's out?"

"Yep. He claims he found Jesus in prison, and he was a model prisoner. He came back to town about a year ago. He's been staying on his property, out southwest of town. We see him now and then when he comes in for supplies, but mostly he stays there."

"What's he do for a living?" Jager asked.

"No idea. Most preppers hunt and fish and do their own gardening, so he's probably living off the land."

Jager started to ask a question, but Woody interrupted him. "Why do you think there's something wrong with your stepdaughter's death?"

"There was something that was just not right." Jager suddenly seemed tired, defeated. "Maybe I'm chasing ghosts. Maybe I'm searching for answers to something that really isn't a question."

I didn't know what to say. People die all the time and sometimes there isn't an answer. I'd learned to view medicine as much of an art as a science. Look at Mother. She was recovering, went to physical therapy, and appeared to be getting stronger. Then she has a heart attack at home and was gone. Was it stress? A weakness in her heart? No one knew.

"What's your gut say?" Woody asked.

"It's a suspicious death," Jager said immediately. "I feel it in my bones."

We were quiet for a minute, absorbing what he said.

"Jake Grimly is the Police Chief now." Woody tapped the picnic table in a staccato rhythm. "Jake is by-the-book. Not very imaginative, but we normally don't get a lot of imaginative crime in Perrault and its surroundings. Drunks, a few hunting accidents, and the occasional prepper who has to be rescued from his own lifestyle."

"I wanted to ask you about that. Preppers? You get them out here?" Jager turned slightly, taking in the CF nearby, the small lake bordering the park, and the bustling town a stone's throw away.

"You're surrounded by the BWCAW," I said. "Lots of room for preppers."

"The what?"

Grandmother chuckled. "You came here to the back of beyond and you don't know where you are?"

He shrugged. "It's somewhat rustic, but I figured it was, you know, limited."

I laughed out loud. "Rustic? You haven't seen rustic. I know some freeholds that would make an outhouse seem like porcelain plumbing."

"Freehold?"

"Inherited property free of any legal or financial entanglements. Some land up here is freehold land. Wulfson lives on a freehold. He inherited from his father." I took pity on Jager's ignorance. "Here. The BWCAW. The Boundary Waters Canoe Area Wilderness. Also known as B-dub. Google it sometime. It's part of the Superior National Forest."

"Now, now. The Superior National Forest is part of the BWCAW." Woody waggled a finger at me.

I smiled. "That's an ongoing debate. Which came first, the forest or the wilderness." I saw Jager's confused expression. "Both are protected national parks. Superior technically came first in designation but B-dub was right behind. There are entry points into the Boundary Waters and permits are required. There's a limit on how many people can enter at one time on any given day."

Woody snorted. "Although it's hard to regulate when there's two million acres of forest, twelve hundred canoe routes, and two thousand campsites with dozens of entry points on lakes and rivers. Not to mention a shared border with Canada at Quetico, and too few forest rangers to track movements."

"The preppers live in the B-dub?" He sounded doubtful.

"On the fringes. We're on the fringe." I pointed northwest. "Six miles that way is an entry point. We sell permits and maps at the store."

"And the gear you need to survive," Grandmother said proudly. "And guides. Because most folks can't find their ass with both hands in a closet with a light on."

Jager raised an expressive eyebrow at this comment.

"And ammo," Woody added.

I nodded. "And ammo. I'd prefer to only sell arrows, but people can take a gun in, so it makes sense to sell the ammo."

"She won't sell guns, though," Grandmother said.

"I would never forgive myself if someone used a weapon that I sold to hurt someone. Although I suppose I'm splitting hairs because I sell ammo and what does it matter if someone got the gun somewhere else? For that matter, selling bows and arrows are just as lethal."

"Don't forget hatchets and grappling hooks," Woody reminded me. "Those could be weapons, too."

"And the way some people cook could be lethal. I am a prime example of that." Grandmother raised her hand. "Can't boil water without burning down the house."

Jager had watched this conversation with little movements of his head, his eyes going from one to the other. He finally came back to me. "The Visit the Wild place on Main Street? I went inside. It's not cheap to get back to nature."

I bristled at his obvious ignorance. "I guess it depends if you want to come back in one piece," I snapped.

Grandmother laughed. "A smart person needs about half of what's sold and could make do without the other half. Reddy's smart to take advantage of the less-than-smart people." She raised her wine cup to me in salute.

And Julie's smart to take advantage of the really dumb ones, I thought glumly. She was making a killing off of gloves priced twice what I carried and climbing rope that cost enough for a small family to eat off for lunch at a better restaurant.

Oh, well. Saving the ignorant from wasting their money was not my problem. My store had a lot of repeat business, and we catered to people who cared more about enjoying the wilderness than appearing good while doing it.

"Sorry. I didn't mean that the way it sounded. I've had my gear paid for by the organization managing my time. First the military and then the police. I forgot how much it can cost to get the right gear for the right situation."

I was mollified by Jager's apology. "I don't know if people realize that the right carabiner or the right canoe can make all the difference."

"Especially on some of those portages," Woody said. "There are some tough trails not far from here. You want the lightest canoe you can get." He tilted his head to study Jager, tapping his wolf's-head cane with one finger. "Army?"

Jager nodded. "82nd Airborne."

"Hmm. Navy here." Woody pursed his lips. "I figured my time on the lakes would give me an edge on the other recruits. Boy, was I wrong. The ocean's a bunch bigger than a lake. But at least I didn't get seasick. I've been on Superior during some big storms, big enough to test a person's stomach."

Grandmother shuddered. "Don't remind me."

Jager gave a brief smile. "Yeah, it seemed cool to parachute into jungles. Grenada showed me how wrong I was."

Woody winced. "I heard that was ugly fighting."

"Yeah, especially for a twenty-year-old kid." Jager stared off in the distance, to the small lake nearby and the trees around it. "I guess this was a wild goose chase," he said softly.

"I wouldn't say that." Woody's lips twitched. "Never underestimate a retired cop."

Jager frowned. "Yeah, maybe."

Woody cocked an eyebrow at him. "You're retired." It was a statement, not a question.

"I tried a desk job, but it didn't work out."

Something in the way he said it made me wonder if that was entirely his choice. He had a tinge of regret or bitterness in his voice.

"And you're not sure what to do now that you're retired." Woody regarded Jager with apparent placidity, but I saw how his sharp eyes took in everything about the stranger.

"I didn't do any post-work planning. Retirement kind of caught me by surprise."

"I've been where you're at. Retirement can sneak up on a man. Let me know if you'd like to chat about it."

"Thanks, but I'm not sure it's the same thing."

"Why? Because I was Chief of Police in a little podunk town, and you were a hotshot detective in the big city?" Woody said it without rancor, and he got a big dose of respect from me for that. I would have chewed Jager out so bad he couldn't walk.

"I'm sorry. I didn't mean—" Jager stopped. "Yeah, I guess I did. Thanks. I'd like to talk to somebody who's been through it."

"Glad to help. Now, about this problem, the one with the accident and Wulfson. You can't go to Jake with this. There's nothing to ask him to examine, only a gut-level feeling that something is off."

"I know. That's the problem."

"Let me do a bit of digging. I help out on cold cases. I'm part of a group that meets online. We read through evidence files and sometimes come up with a new angle on old cases. Can you stick around for a few days? I'll see what I find," Woody said thoughtfully. "This is exactly the kind of thing my guys like to poke at."

"I'd appreciate it. I don't want to go back and tell Candy I didn't find anything. I want to at least put her mind at ease and tell her we checked all angles."

"And put your mind at ease," I said.

He seemed surprised. "Yeah. You're right. Mindy was my daughter for a time. I want to know what happened. If anything."

Woody pulled a dog-eared memo pad out of his back pocket and jotted some numbers. "This is my phone number, both at the CF and my mobile. Where are you staying?"

"Echo Shores Lodge. I have a room for the next few days."

Woody slid the piece of paper across the table to me and I slid it over to Jager. "We have our regular Zoom meeting tonight. I'll run some ideas by the group. There's a bunch of folks from different parts of the country. Maybe somebody's come across something that might trigger an idea."

Jager pocketed the paper and stood, leaning briefly on the table to help himself upright. "I appreciate it. Thanks for listening to me. I'll give you a call tomorrow."

He turned to me. "And thanks for educating me about the B-dub and the locals." He walked away, going back to his car.

"That was odd," Grandmother said. "Do you think someone had anything to do with the young woman's death?"

Woody gathered up the detritus of his shared meal. "The guy's a cop. Cops develop an instinct about things like this."

"But why would someone do that? Why kill her?" I shook my head. "I think he's grasping at straws. Sometimes people, you know, they die."

"Maybe," Woody agreed. "But I still say you have to trust a cop's instincts."

I didn't argue with him, but I wondered if Woody wasn't identifying with Mr. Jager and his problems. Well, time would tell, I suppose. I escorted Grandmother to Woody's golf cart and saw her safely inside then watched them shoot away, Grandmother shouting and waving her hand in good-bye. Jager had driven off and I went to my car, driving to my small house nestled in the woods outside of town.

When Doug and I bought the house, we were one of three homes on the narrow road that overlooked Lake Shawatok, north of town. Three more homes had joined us, separated by thick stands of trees and the contours of the land. My neighbors to the east helped me with some of the heavier chores such as log-splitting and tree removal, but generally the neighbors kept to themselves and each of us was self-sufficient with our various small snow tractors that doubled as lawnmowers in the summer.

My house was the first one on the left with a sloping drive to the house proper. The lake shimmered in the distance, separated from me by a steep embankment and a heavy stand of maples and oaks. I drove into the garage and exited, scurrying into the kitchen where warmth and my enormous tabby cat, Hoody, greeted me.

I topped up Hoody's kibble bowl, gave him a treat, then went into the living room to start a fire in the fireplace. My house was small with four rooms downstairs (kitchen, dining, den, and living) and two bedrooms upstairs under the slanting eaves. A tiny basement and a powder room near the kitchen and a full bath upstairs completed the arrangement. It was the right size for me, small and compact and easy to keep maintained and cleaned.

I busied myself with sorting through mail, checking my email on my computer in the den, and finally sank onto my couch in front of the fire with a cocoa spiked with chocolate liqueur at around nine o'clock. A typical evening for me. I seldom turned on the TV in the corner of the room, preferring instead to read or listen to a book on my iPad.

I slung my legs up on the hassock and tossed an old lap robe over my lower half. I loved that old blanket. Mother made it for me, and it had snags and sags in its crocheted surface. Hoody paced over and snuggled next to me and soon I was lying back, letting a narrator carry me away in a thriller set in the depths of Egypt. This particular author had a penchant for the macabre and I grimaced at some of the gory details.

The fire had died by the time I unwound myself from cat and couch and made my rounds, checking the back door and front door locks. I went up to bed, yawning and almost stumbling over Hoody when he darted ahead to reach his spot on my queen-sized bed. I soon joined him and dropped into sleep immediately, puffy bedspread tugged close to my face.

Something woke me hours later. Hoody was sitting up, staring at the open door to my bedroom. I checked my clock. Two in the morning. The noise came again. Now I sat up, heart hammering. Someone was rattling the knob on either the front or back door. Whoever it was, they weren't being stealthy.

I grabbed my trusty baseball bat, kept under the bed for this purpose. I peered through the dormer window but didn't see anyone below me in front. I had no windows facing the back on this floor, so I ran down the staircase as stealthily as I could, following the white tip of Hoody's tail ahead of me. I came into the front foyer. The front doorknob wasn't moving. I checked out the side windows. Nothing.

I peeked around the corner in the den, which gave me a clear view through the kitchen to the back door. No sound and no movement. I inched forward cautiously, tiptoeing through the den and into the kitchen. I sidled to the back door and peeked out.

I saw movement on the terrace above the lake. It appeared to be human—two legs and a torso—but the shifting clouds against the almost-full moon made it hard to tell for sure. It might have been an errant moose or deer. I waited a few minutes, but the figure merged with the shadows. I double-checked the lock then checked the downstairs windows to be sure. I went back upstairs and tried to get back to sleep.

It took a while before I was able to slip into dreamland, visions of Egypt mingling with the trees around my house.

Chapter 3

I woke at six, the way I always did. I considered the previous evening's scare. Had someone actually tried to break in? If someone wanted to get in, there were several windows that could be easily broken to gain entry. Why rattle the doorknob?

I pulled on my exercise clothes and went downstairs, picking up my iPad to select a workout video for the day. Maybe it was that damn thriller I listened to. It had a detailed scene of someone breaking into a home. Had I mistakenly heard a noise and translated it into part of the plot?

It was too dark to go outside and check around, so I went to the basement for my morning routine. My exercise space was one big open room, unfinished with pipes and beams above. The furnace and water heater sat in one corner and my treadmill and weights were in the opposite corner, the weights on a remnant of thick carpet to provide some protection against the cement floor's chill.

I dialed up a half-hour of weightlifting on my fitness app and was soon struggling to follow the enthusiastic and buff young people manhandling their weights on the iPad. I was in relatively good shape, but aches and pains were creeping up on me, exacerbated by the brutally cold weather we usually had between November and April. I figured if I kept moving in some way, shape, or form I might keep old age at bay.

As I lifted and sweated, I thought about Mother and Grandmother. Both women had exercised most of their lives, usually with daily brisk walks outside or at the gym in bad weather as well as other forms of exertion. Mother had participated in a Senior Aerobics Class three times a week and Grandmother took dance classes for as long as I could remember. She and Woody could still put others to shame at the local bar when we went out weekly for our Friday Funday outing.

Thoughts of Mother made me think about the accident and its aftermath and of Jager. Could Boyd Wulfson have anything to do with a young woman's death? Even as I considered it, I dismissed it. Wulfson had been in prison for a little more than four years. Because of our past altercations, I had a restraining order against him. I'd been notified when he was released from prison and again when he returned to town. But I hadn't seen him except from a distance and that was only once or twice.

I was certain that Jager was searching for an answer that wasn't in Perrault, Minnesota. My doorbell ringing coincided with my online fitness trainer saying, "Good work, team! Now take a minute for a cooldown. You earned it!"

"No shit," I muttered, wiping sweat off my face. Today's workout had strained my aging body to its limits. I staggered up the steps and went to the front door to check the peephole. G.C. Jager was on my stoop, shoulders hunched against the brisk wind.

I debated opening the door. How did he find out where I lived? Then I realized that any phone book would have my address if he could find a phone book anywhere. For that matter, the folks at the Lodge could point him to my house. I had a reciprocal agreement with them. They referred tourists to me, and I recommended their lodge for people to stay overnight before taking off on the hiking adventures planned by my team.

"You're out and about early," I said when I opened the door.

He seemed abashed. "Oh, wow. Yeah. I didn't even think about the time. I'm sorry." He eyed my sweaty workout gear. "I guess I didn't wake you up."

I dabbed at my face. "Nope. I just finished a half-hour with an online trainer." I stood to one side. "Come on in. I'm making coffee. Care for a cup?"

"Sure. Here's your paper." He held out the Sunday paper in its flimsy plastic wrapping.

"Thanks." He followed me into the house. I pointed to the coat rack near the door, and he slipped out of his jacket. It was the same tweedy-looking sport coat as yesterday. Today he wore a pale blue sweater over a dark shirt with dark blue jeans. The blue of the sweater matched his eyes.

I went to the right of the staircase, through my den to the kitchen. "How'd you find me? This street is off the beaten path." I dropped the newspaper in the dining room and rejoined him near the counter.

"The lodge people told me where you lived. One of your fishing guides was working the front desk this morning."

I ran through a list of people in my mind. "Willy Grimm?" I asked.

Jager nodded. "He said he didn't have much work right now, at least until the ice is thick enough. Do people really go out on the ice to fish?"

I laughed. "Stick around. In another six weeks the lake will be covered with ice shacks." I gestured to the windows overlooking the lake. I stared more intently at my back terrace. A thick layer of frost covered the stone pavers. They appeared crisscrossed with tracks but from here it was hard to tell what kind, whether human or animal.

Jager joined me. "You've had company."

"Yeah, somebody rattled the doorknob last night." I pointed to the door that led outside and thus to the garage. "Maybe it was some kids trying to spook me." I managed a chuckle. "They succeeded."

He went from the door to the window. "In order to get in here and rattle the doorknob somebody had to come around the house. Your garage blocks egress because of the fence you have enclosing the back yard."

"Yep. I couldn't fence in the entire yard, but I figured I'd slow any critters on the garage side at least." I frowned at the mushy-appearing patio. The snow/frost was already starting to melt away. "Whoever it was, they weren't trying to be quiet. I heard the noise upstairs."

"You're isolated out here. There aren't any streetlights."

"Heck, we only got curb and gutter two years ago. It used to be a lane." I turned to the coffeepot. I was still disturbed by last night's event but not sure what I could do about it. "I'll swing by the police station on my way to work. Maybe other people have had similar things happen to them."

I glanced at him, wondering if he'd comment because he was a cop, albeit retired. But he was staring at the back patio, his face thoughtful.

"Have a seat." I busied myself with the coffeepot

and mugs, getting out cream and sugar in case he wanted it. Then I led the way through the curved entryway into the dining room and took a seat at my small four-seater table.

He followed me and sat opposite. "Why don't you go to a gym? I'm curious," he hastened to add. "I used to use the gym at the precinct and I'm trying to figure out if I want to join a gym or not. I'm still new to the retirement frame of mind."

I gulped some water and dabbed at my mouth when I dribbled. Working out always got me dehydrated. "We have a couple of gyms in town, but I don't like working out with other people around me. Some people use the gym as a place to meet people."

I wrinkled my nose. "I'm not into that. Besides, I don't need other people critiquing my form. I had a rather unpleasant experience in the gym and it kinda turned me off. Although maybe I'm being too egocentric. I doubt if anyone would even stare at me. I mentioned that to my mother once and she said, 'Rebeka Evelyn Danforth, why do you think you're the center of the universe?' "

The memory washed over me. "I miss her," I whispered.

"From what people have said, your mother was a beloved woman. Some folks at the lodge mentioned her. My parents died years ago when I was in the Army. I envy your relationship with your grandmother. My grandfather is still alive, but he disowned me when I joined the police. We haven't spoken in decades."

"Really? Why disown you? What's so wrong about being a cop?"

Jager peered around the room, avoiding my gaze.

"He wanted me to go into the family business. I didn't want to."

"What business?" I gulped some more water and choked when he said,

"Jager Pharmaceuticals."

I dabbed at more dribbles. "Wow. That's like, the biggest drug company on the Left Coast."

One corner of his mouth quirked up in a smile. "Left Coast."

"Yeah, there's the Right Coast, the Left Coast, Flyover Land, and BFN. You're in BFN."

"BFN?"

Bum Fuck Nowhere, I thought. "Big Fat Nowhere," I said. "Anyway, back to exercising. I'd rather do it at home when I feel like it, not on a business schedule. And, like I said, I don't want to go to a gym and have people watch my fat wobble around."

He looked me up and down. "Not much fat that I can see."

"Enough to be annoying." I eyed him. If he was joking, he was hiding it. "You appear fit as a fiddle for a man who was recently injured. Hmm. That's an odd expression. I wonder where it came from."

"It's from Britain, in the 1600s. It doesn't mean healthy. It's more that something is suitable for its purpose."

I gaped at him. "And you know that how?"

"My ex-wife. She was—she is—an Elizabethan scholar. Shakespeare and all that."

"Candy?"

"She goes by Candace when she's teaching." He wiggled his eyebrows. "It's more impressive to college freshmen."

"I see the point."

We sat in companionable silence while sunlight wended its way into the room. Hoody wandered in to check the stranger. Jager leaned over to give the cat a head rub. "That's a big cat." Hoody flopped into the pool of sun and began languid bathing.

"Yeah, Hoody's a monster, all right. My store clerk, Rhea Hood, gave him to me so I named him after them and because of that black patch on his head and cheeks. It's like he's wearing a hood." I tilted my head and regarded the feline. "And he's tough like a hood, I guess. She found him abandoned on the lakeshore about five years ago. He was living on scraps and mice."

"He's landed in a happy place." Jager's gaze lingered on the corner display cabinet where several pictures were positioned. "You look like your father." He went to the cabinet for a closer view.

"I inherited Daddy's hair and Mother's physique. I like to think I'm small but mighty, like she was." I heard the coffee machine making its puck-puck noise which told me it was wrapping up the brewing cycle. I pushed away from the table and went to the kitchen.

"You said she died a few years ago?" he asked, leaving the pictures behind and following me.

"October 7. Three years ago."

"What a coincidence. Mindy died on October 7 two years ago."

"That is weird." I poured coffee into my Prince mug, the one with the quote *Dearly beloved, we are gathered here today to get through this thing called life.* I handed it to him and poured another for me in my Eric Clapton World Tour mug.

Jager examined the mug. "I toured Prince's home

when I was in the Cities. "Purple Rain." One of my favorite songs."

I raised my mug in salute. "Right up there with "Layla.""

"Great minds think alike." He gently clicked his mug against mine. "I was wondering if you'd like to go out for breakfast. I admit, I'm kind of at loose ends. I wanted to pick your brain about ways to approach Wulfson. I still think I need to talk to him."

I thought he'd be foolish to do so, but I didn't voice that opinion again. Let the man hold out some hope that crazy Boyd Wulfson would give him the time of day, much less answers. I gestured to the sugar and cream, but he shook his head.

"Sure, I'd like that. I have time this morning. The store's open from ten to two on Sunday with winter hours. Reed is working today, and he'll open, and I need to be there by eleven to interview someone for our open clerk position. Reed's wife is my regular person, but she was hurt in an accident, and she's laid up for the winter."

I ran a hand over my saggy gym shorts and T-shirt. "I need to clean up before I can go anywhere."

"If you'd like me to come back at a more reasonable hour, I can," Jager volunteered.

"What? No, that's okay. It'll only take me a minute." I gestured to the dining room. "Feel free to sort out the paper for me."

"I meant if you're not comfortable having me stay here while you get ready, I can leave."

What a gentlemanly thing to do. "That's okay. I'll lock the bathroom door." I winked to show I was kidding. "I read the Metro section first and you can put the ads in a separate pile." I didn't wait for his reply but took my coffee and headed for the stairs.

I made a mental note to check on Rhea and see how she was doing. Reed and Rhea Hood were in their early forties with two teenagers who also helped at the store during busy times. R&R (as they were known) had worked at the store almost from Day One. Rhea was injured when out jogging a few weeks earlier. The driver sped away and left her by the side of the road with fractured ribs and a broken left leg.

I scampered upstairs and showered quickly, blow-drying my hair to give it some fluff. I dressed in my usual work uniform of jeans and a yellow polo shirt under a Visit the Wild V-neck sweatshirt in dark gold. I dabbed on some powder, eye shadow and mascara and returned to find Jager staring through the patio door in the dining room.

"It might have been coyotes," I said, joining him to evaluate the faint line of tracks. "Not wolves, though."

"Wolves? You get them here?"

"Sure. They normally don't come this close to people. Coyotes are noisy and make sure you know they're around. Wolves are sneaky." I leaned over and tapped Hoody's head. "This guy never goes outside, or he'd be a snack." The cat shot me a disgusted expression as though to say, 'hey, I can take care of myself.'

"This is a whole different world," Jager murmured. "I'm used to crackheads and thieves."

I laughed. "Coyotes are thieves and I swear wolves act like crackheads sometimes. I guess we have the four-legged variety, not the two-legged kind. Well, we'd better get going so we can beat the Baptists."

"What?" He regarded me quizzically.

I laughed. "My mother used to say that. Whenever

you go out to eat on a Sunday, you need to time your arrival at a restaurant so you can beat the church crowd."

"Man, I am a dope, aren't I? I completely forgot it was Sunday, and you might go to church."

I led the way through the dining room to the living room. "No worries. I'm not a churchgoer and never have been. I'll lead and you can follow me to the restaurant, okay? I need to go to the store after we eat and I'm not sure when I'll wrap up there. We can go to Gil's. It's a bar but they do a good breakfast there and very few Baptists show up."

"Sounds good." He slipped on his coat and left through the front door. I locked up behind him then went to the back door, pulling on my coat and exiting, making sure to lock up behind me. I went into the garage and backed out my small SUV, taking the lead on the quiet street.

While I drove to town, I mentally mapped out my day. It was now almost eight. That gave us a leisurely hour or so to have breakfast. Maybe a Bloody Mary would be in my future. I grinned at the thought. Then I'd head to the store and meet the young woman who had applied for the temporary clerk job. I needed to review her application and resume before we talked.

It was unusual for a young person to be available in the wintertime to work. Most of the late teens-to-mid-twenties workers were in college or otherwise hired elsewhere. I had several part-timers who worked for us in the summer, but they normally weren't available after Labor Day. This woman had recently moved to town and said in her application that she was interested in working for a woman-owned business. There weren't many of us in town.

I made a left turn off Main Street and parked behind Gil's Tavern in the town parking lot. Jager pulled in beside me. He was driving a rental, a medium-sized dark sedan. I saw the rental company logo on the back window. We met at the front of our cars.

"Why do the fire hydrants have flags?" Jager pointed to the hydrant on the side of the street.

"That way they can find them in the snow." I glanced at him when no acknowledgement was forthcoming. He appeared skeptical. "Trust me. We get major snow here. Once the plows come through some of the drifts are taller than me." I snorted. "Of course, a lot of things are taller than me."

He held the back door open. "You must get lost during a big storm."

"Nah, I hunker down at home and wait for it to pass." I entered the dark interior of the bar, traversing the long rear hallway to emerge into the brighter-lit main room. I waved to Gil who was behind the bar, working on some kind of orange juice drink.

"Hey, Reddy!" he called out. "Good to see you!"

I waved then pulled off my coat with the bright red hood, tucking my lightweight gloves into the pockets.

"You don't wear blaze orange?" Jager asked. "Isn't it essential here after October 1? You know, one of those rules like don't wear white after Labor Day." He didn't smile when he said it, but his blue eyes laughed at me.

I twitched the edge of the coat to show camo fabric with neon green stripes. "Depends on where I am. In the woods I turn it inside out. Camo and blaze orange aren't a fashion choice here, they're a necessity." I slung the coat over the back of my chair. "Firearms season starts in early November. We're in archery season right now

50

for deer."

"Don't forget bear season. We still have a few days for that since the permit area is about a mile outside of town." Gilly, Gil's wife and the waitress for Sunday, had appeared at our table, menus in hand. "Coffee to start you?" She brandished the coffee pot in her left hand.

"Sure." I set the menu aside. I knew it by heart.

Jager studied the grimy laminated page while Gilly fetched two heavy ceramic mugs with Gil's logo, a tipsy-appearing buck, on them. She poured the coffee, shooting Jager covertly curious glances.

"Give me a Bloody Mary, light on the spice and the number 4." I tapped the menu.

"Over easy and wheat?" Gilly asked, scribbling on her notepad.

"Yep. Same as usual. I'm a creature of habit."

"Ditto on the Bloody Mary and the number 6 with pancakes." Jager waited for her to finish jotting then handed her our menus.

"You got it, folks." She sashayed away, her ample hips swinging.

Jager peered around curiously. Several tables were occupied, mainly with men, probably hunters either going out or coming in. We typically got more people for firearms than archery. The room was 'decorated' with assorted beer signs and posters for alcohol. The long bar was dark wood with several gouges along its sides and the surface.

"There are a couple of other spots in town for breakfast, but Gil makes a mean Bloody Mary," I confided. "It's got the right amount of kick to it."

"This place reminds me of a bar not far from my precinct back in the city. Not long on décor but the food is great."

"You're a long way from home, Mr. Jager." I checked behind me at the front door, whose bell rang when three men in camo came in.

"Gideon."

I swung around to face him. "I beg your pardon?"

"My name. It's Gideon."

"Oh, well, yes. Thank you." Why was I thanking him for sharing his name? I must be losing my mind. "Like I said, this is a far cry from San Francisco."

"It's an interesting change of pace, that's for sure. I've never stayed long in such a small town. I get the feeling everybody knows everybody here."

"Only because they do. It's different in the summertime when we get the hikers and campers coming through. But things get quiet in the fall until November when the deer hunters come out in force."

"I saw another store like yours. It recently opened. Competition?"

I tried to smile but it might have come out more like a grimace. "Yeah, you might say that. My ex-husband's ex-wife opened it. Turns out she learned the business from Doug then turned around when they got divorced and decided to go into business for herself." The ungrateful, sneaky little bitch.

"Clever name for a store. Dip Your Oar."

"She's a clever girl," I muttered.

"It seemed really upscale."

"You went in?"

"Yeah, I figured I'd scope out the town. She had some pricy stuff."

"She's more upscale. We're more utilitarian." I gnawed on my lip, a nagging worry in the back of my mind. What was Julie up to? I knew I couldn't compete with her inventory.

Jager sipped his coffee, his eyes on me. "I'm sorry, but—your hair. It's such an unusual color." His cheeks flushed. "I admit, I wondered if it might be artificial but then I saw that picture of your father."

"Titian," I said. "Brown-red-gold. Another reason I'm called Reddy. Not only my initials."

"Initials?"

"Rebeka Evelyn Danforth. My grandmother is Rose Elizabeth Davis, and my mother was Ruth Ellen Duffy."

"That's amazing. Three women in the same family with the same initials."

"I was accused of marrying Doug Danforth because of his last name," I admitted. "But that's not why I married him. Truth be told, I'm not sure why I did." That reminded me of Jager's relationship with his ex. "I'm sorry about the loss of your stepdaughter. I think it's great that you and she stayed so close after the divorce."

"Candy was good about it. And Joe, her current husband, was, too. Candy's first husband died of cancer and then I came along. Mindy and Jason were young and going through all kinds of stuff because of their dad's death. I feel like I had a hand in raising them. Mindy and I both loved to go to baseball games."

His expression softened. "I can't tell you how many we went to together. I was sorry to see them move away from the Bay area. Candy got a great job offer and between that and Joe's job, well, they had to move. Candy and Joe are a great couple. I envy them. It's like they were meant to be together. It's not fair that Mindy didn't get a chance to live her life. She was so young."

"No one should have their life cut short. It's good of

you to help."

"I'm in a position to help so I want to do it."

"What do you mean?"

"Hmm?"

"What position?"

"Oh. Retirement and all." He said it as though he was facing the guillotine.

"Lucky you," I said with deliberate perkiness.

"Yeah."

"You don't sound pleased about it."

He shrugged. "I never considered it much. I didn't think much about being old."

"Age doesn't equal retirement, you know." I didn't understand his gloomy mood. "Consider me. I had sufficient funds, and I could have retired, but I decided to do something I love to do. And I'm throwing a monkey wrench at my ex-husband, I do admit."

"You are? How?"

"Doug and I started Visit the Wild when we were first married. I took sole ownership when we divorced. Doug kept the business in Duluth and renamed it Romancing the Wild." I smirked. "Romantic adventures in the northern woods. Sounds great but sometimes the reality is a bit buggier and smellier."

Jager nodded agreement. "Especially if you're camping."

"Well, his clients don't camp. They glamp. But there's still a bit of competition between us even though my store is more about roughing it." I sipped my coffee. "You said you were in the police for a long time."

"Yeah. Thirty years. I was injured on the job about seven years ago. A bullet took out a chunk of my thigh. It was bad enough that I didn't feel like I should be in the field anymore. I shifted to Cyber Crimes, but it wasn't the same. Tracking down electronic criminals isn't the same as chasing 'em on foot or in a car. I decided it was time to pack it in."

It sounded like he was still unhappy about that decision. Further talk was curtailed when Gil approached the table, our Bloody Mary drinks in hand.

"Hey, Gil." I eyed my drink, tall and frosty with a rim of salt and a skewer of olives sticking out. "Is this your usual awesome wake-me-up?"

"I aim to please." He leaned closer to me. "When's the next outing going?" he asked in a low voice.

"Next week. I have three going out. Why?" I looked around. "Ozzy?"

"You know how he is. You gotta keep him busy, Reddy."

"He'll be busy next week. I'll give him the four-day trip." I glanced at Jager. "Ozzy's a great guide but he tends to love his beer. When he's on-duty, he's great. Off-duty, he's, well, really off-duty."

Gil took up the story. "When the mines started laying off, men didn't know what to do. Most of 'em had gone into the mines right out of high school. Not everybody's cut out for a gig on the big lake, so we got drifters. Ozzy drifted into town and somehow stayed." Gil shook his head mournfully and moved to the next table to chat with the men sitting there.

"Can you interpret that for me?" Jager asked.

"Sure. Taconite mining used to be big in this area. There were three large iron ranges, but now only one is still in operation. That's why this whole area is called the Iron Range. When mines started to fold some miners tried maritime sailing on Lake Superior, but it's a tough field to break into. Remember that song, "The Wreck of the Edmund Fitzgerald"? Big ships still traverse the Great Lakes out of Duluth and Superior, about forty miles that way." I jerked a thumb over my shoulder. "Some of the ex-miners found spots as guides. Ozzy's one of them."

"I imagine it's not everyone who can fit in here." He sipped the Bloody Mary, eyes opening wide when he sampled its punch. "It's a unique part of the world."

"I think many areas in the country are as unique. You only have to find them, like you did. You would never have stumbled on us if a mystery hadn't brought you here."

"I'm glad it did." His gaze swept over the diverse crowd. "I've been wondering about where I might land."

"Here?" I shook my head. "Don't say that until you've gone through at least one winter. That might convince you otherwise."

We focused on our drinks for a minute or two then he said, "You and your grandmother are close."

"She, Mother, and I were always doing things together. My father died when I was young and my grandfather—" I raised my hands. "He ran away a long time ago. It was us three women."

"But you were married. Did your husband mind? That you were so close."

"Doug? No, I think he was relieved. He was always unfaithful." I frowned. "That's odd. I never thought of in those terms before. Unfaithful. He did not keep faith with our vows. Anyway, I think it gave him the excuse he needed to find the next pretty young thing to keep him happy."

"You sound as though you've forgiven him. It's in

the past."

"Yes, it is. Forgive him?" I considered that. "Yes, he hurt me, but he hurt my pride, mainly. No one wants to be considered old and useless at any age. I was forty-four and that's a vulnerable age for a woman. You're right on the cusp of menopause, you've become invisible, and now your husband affirms your crone status by leaving you for a younger woman." I sighed.

"Invisible? What does that mean?"

"Before a certain age, a woman is seen. Maybe not all women, but most women are. We're always conscious of being evaluated, being judged, usually by men but sometimes by other women who see us as rivals. It's subtle but it's there. But once a woman hits a certain age, she's no longer visible. It's like we've become a part of the scenery. We're no longer sex objects. We're just people."

He sipped his drink, considering what I said. "You're not invisible."

"Ah, but I am. I'm at the magic age of fifty and over the hill to most men."

He nodded. "Yeah. To most men." He turned his head and stared into my eyes. "Not to all men."

I had a hard time swallowing. "I guess if a guy notices me then he's a keeper."

He smiled. "I hope so."

What was I seeing in those cool blue eyes of his?

Chapter 4

Before I could evaluate his intent, our food arrived. I was relieved. I had no desire to get entangled with someone who was only in town for a day or two.

Entangled? Who was I kidding? The guy was being nice. We took our time with our meal, savoring the drinks and finishing up with another cup of coffee. It was past nine-thirty by the time we left the bar.

"I think we beat the Baptists," Gideon said, nodding to the church down the street. People were streaming out from the early service, always held at eight o'clock so hunters and fishermen could have their dose of religion before going out to bag some unsuspecting critter.

As I turned back to talk to him, I saw Julie, Doug's ex, on the sidewalk outside her storefront speaking with someone. They were barely visible between two buildings.

"That's worrisome," I muttered.

"What?" Gideon followed my gaze.

"That's Julie Billings. She owns the store we were talking about. And that's Ron. He's brother to my store manager."

"She's your ex-husband's ex-wife, right?"

"Yep. She retained her maiden name. I wonder if she's poaching."

"What do you mean?"

"Ron does some guide work for me. In fact, he's one

of the most requested guides we have." I narrowed my eyes, glaring at the two people who were oblivious of my regard.

"Is he married?"

"What? No."

"Then it isn't poaching. I think it's a bit of flirting."

I cast a surreptitious peek past Gideon. Maybe he was right. "Ron's about the right age for her, I guess. And he's not a bad looking guy." I sighed. "I'm overthinking it. There are other outfitters in town. Why do I have competition on the brain?"

"Maybe because you have a history with her. I don't think you have anything to worry about. I was wondering…" He gave me a hopeful glance. "Would you have time later today to show me where the accident happened? I realize it might reawaken some painful memories, but I'd like to see it. I have no idea if Mrs. Wulfson has anything to do with Mindy's death, but it might be smart for me to see the location before I talk to him. Make myself familiar with the scene, I guess. Once a cop, always a cop."

"Sure, we can." I glanced at my fitness gadget which doubled as a wristwatch. "It's almost ten now. I should be done at the store by one o'clock or so. I don't plan to eat lunch after that breakfast."

"Ditto. I may need a nap."

"Why don't you come to the store at one? You can leave your car there and I can drive us to the site."

"Thanks. I appreciate it. I'm kind of at loose ends here. Maybe your grandmother's friend will be able to find something."

"Woody? If anybody can find a needle in a haystack, it's Woodrow Wilson Hunter. He's tenacious. He's been keeping time with Grandmother for almost ten years. He asks her to marry him every year on the anniversary of their first date. She keeps saying no."

"That is tenacity. Why won't she marry him?"

I snorted. "She wants to be free to play the field."

He tilted his head back and laughed. "I admire her optimism," he said when his laughter died.

"I do, too. I try to emulate her but she's a tough act to follow." I started walking to my car and he fell into step with me.

"Thanks for going out for breakfast with me. I'm a stranger in a strange land here. It's nice to have a guide."

"Thanks for asking me." I paused by my car. "I'll see you in a few hours then."

"I appreciate you taking the time to help out." He touched my arm then went to his car, parked behind mine.

I slid into the driver's seat and drove the four blocks to my store, parking in back next to Reed's ancient Subaru SUV. He refused to trade it in. 'Only a hundred thousand miles,' he'd say. 'It's just starting to warm up.'

His wife, Rhea, confided in me that she was happy he loved the old heap. 'He's content and that's fine with me. Better that than he has to buy a new truck every time he turns around.'

I entered through the back door, hanging my coat on the hook there. My office was to the right, a small space with enough room for my desk and chair, a guest chair, a four-drawer filing cabinet, and a small bookshelf.

"Hey, Reed," I called out.

"Hey yourself," he called back.

I sank into my stylish new nylon desk chair and took Barbara Forester's application from the filing bin on my desk. The young woman had retail experience in the Twin Cities, working at one of the big box outfitters. She was nineteen with one year of community college behind her. That apparently was enough because she decided it wasn't for her.

The address she listed was in nearby Shore's Point, a tiny community nestled on the far side of the lake and comprised of two bars, a few houses, and one sad-looking gas station. In my opinion, no one would deliberately choose to live there so she must have been a local who returned home.

The application form had the standard fields to fill in plus several that had to do with camping, fishing, and hunting. The woman appeared to be well versed in gun use, fishing gear, and camping equipment. There was a notation that she had done firearms instruction and led fishing courses for women.

She even had a Guide Permit and Wilderness First Aid certification plus had taken a Wilderness First Aid class through NOLS, a global wilderness group that trained outdoor leaders. That surprised me because those kinds of Wilderness Preparedness classes were not cheap.

I wondered what her long-term plans were. I paid a good wage, and we had health benefits and profit-sharing. Many of my guides had been with me for years, as had Rhea and Reed. I could use additional help in the store seasonally, but I wasn't sure I could offer her anything once Rhea came back on staff full-time. Well, I'd talk it over with her and see what she said.

I went into the main store area where Reed was chatting with a customer. The man was interested in winter outings and Reed was going over our small catalog with him. I busied myself with inventory, sorting through items I wanted to put on sale. Reed joined me when the customer left.

"How's Rhea doing?" I asked. "I've been meaning to stop by and see her, but I hate to bother her if she's not up for company."

"She's coming along but it's slow. I sure wish I knew who slammed into her." Reed's long, somewhat homely face, darkened into a scowl. "I'd let them know what I think."

"It was probably some kid, and he panicked. Although I have to admit, it's pretty brazen to hit somebody and then drive away."

"The police don't have any idea who might have done it. They said there should be some kind of indication on the front fender of the car that hit her, but they haven't found any cars showing that kind of damage." He scowled as he sorted through clothing, moving items to one side for our clearance sale. "At least she's not in pain anymore. Now it's only a big inconvenience. She's getting the hang of the crutches, and she gets around pretty good."

My cell phone, sunk into my back jeans pocket, chimed the opening bars of Glen Miller's "Tuxedo Junction," one of Grandmother's favorite songs. I moved to the long checkout counter, pulling out my phone as I went.

"Hi, Grandmother. How's your Sunday going?"

"It's rather nice today. We had cinnamon rolls for breakfast. A nice change of pace from the gruel they usually serve."

I laughed. "The food there isn't bad, and you know it."

"I heard that you and Mr. Jager had breakfast together." Grandmother sounded smug, as though she'd caught me out in a faux pas.

"Gideon," I said absently, sorting through the price tags on the counter.

"Gideon?"

"That's his name. Yes, we did. He's coming by the store later today and we're going out to the accident site. He'd like to see where it happened."

"Hmm. Two dates in one day. It sounds serious, dear."

"They aren't dates," I protested. Reed caught my attention, holding up a dark green hoody. I shook my head and gestured to the Sale rack.

"I think they're dates. I saw the way he watched you yesterday."

Now she had my attention. Grandmother was an extremely perceptive person, often correctly interpreting the behavior of others that had totally stumped me.

"What do you mean?" I asked.

"I mean you need to take advantage of his interest. Life is finite, my dear. Enjoy it while you can." She sighed. "I've certainly enjoyed my life, and I want you to have as much fun as I did. As I still am, for that matter, given the infirmities and indignities of old age."

"He lives in California. I live in Northern Minnesota. I doubt whether there's any future in his interest."

"All I'm saying is for you to enjoy it while you can. Things tend to work out in ways you could never anticipate."

"Speaking of things working out, I heard from one of my suppliers. They have a new line of backpacks in stock. They wondered if I wanted to see it. How do you feel about a day trip to Duluth on Wednesday?"

"I think that's a marvelous idea. What time?"

"I'll pick you up around nine or so. We can have lunch there."

"Perfect. I'll look forward to it. See you then. And say hello to Gideon for me." She rang off before I could comment. Not that any comment I made would make any difference to her opinion. Grandmother was a woman of strong convictions.

I continued my sorting and pricing until eleven when the door opened, and a young woman walked in. She was smaller than I expected. I'm not sure why I was anticipating someone much beefier, but Barb Forester was a short woman, about my height, which was a bit over five feet tall. She had a stocky build, and I could tell she had some muscles from the way her long-sleeved turtleneck hugged her arms in her sleeveless puffy vest.

"Are you Barb?" I asked, coming out from behind the counter. She nodded and I held out my hand. "I'm Rebeka Danforth. Come on back and we'll chat." I gestured to the rear of the store and my office there.

"I've always admired your store," she said when she took the one guest chair facing my desk.

"You have? Why?" I pulled her application toward me and tugged my notepad closer.

"It's a woman-owned business in a man's world. I admire that." She regarded me with frank interest from dark brown eyes. Her hair, chin-length and straight, was parted in the middle, her bangs framing her dark eyebrows. It wasn't a particularly attractive hairstyle, but it was certainly utilitarian. She was deeply tanned, both hands and face. Barb Forester exuded an air of calm competence, as though her current mood was curious, not concerning.

"Tell me about yourself," I suggested. "It appears you have a great deal of wilderness experience. Do you live in the area? Have you done some hunting or fishing?"

Her hands, clasped in her lap, shifted to reclasp in a different position. It was the only sign of nervousness she showed. "I moved away when I was younger, but I came back to this area two years ago. As I indicated on the application, I tried taking some community college courses. I wanted to go into nursing. My adoptive mother is a nurse. I took some classes, but I decided it wasn't for me. I'm taking a break and thinking about what to do."

"Tell me about your retail experience in the Cities." I glanced at the application and when I looked up again, she was watching me with a wary, expectant expression.

That faded when she began to speak in a low, even voice. She recited the dates she'd been employed and talked about the challenges of working in a big city in an outdoor store.

"It's hard to identify with an urbanite who wants the whole 'outdoor experience.' " She designated the last two words with air quotes. "I've never been an urban person and never will."

"We get plenty of city people here," I pointed out. "People here on vacation."

"But your store is more for the serious camper, the serious outdoor person. It's not like that new store down the street." Forester jerked her chin to indicate where Julie's store was located, somewhere behind me. "That's for the wannabes." She said it without inflection, but I heard a trace of amusement.

I went through the other previous employments on her application. She mentioned several incidents where she had to work with difficult or indecisive customers.

"It's difficult for people to describe what they want when they've never done it before," she finished. "It's like a guessing game sometimes."

"If you're willing to spend the time, it can be done. What are your plans for the future?"

"I'll be honest. I want something to get me through the winter. In the spring I'll decide what my next step will be. I'm not sure if I should go back to school or maybe travel a bit and go out west." She smiled faintly. "It depends on how the winter plays out, I guess."

That coincided with what I needed. I gave her the details about the starting wage, benefits, and policies in the store. They seemed acceptable. At the end of the half-hour, I pushed away from the desk and held out my hand again. "I'd like to offer you the position."

She appeared surprised. "Aren't you going to call my references or check on my employment history?"

"I've already done that. It's one of the first things I do when I get an application. There's no reason to ask a person for an interview if the details on their application don't pan out. Come with me. I'll introduce you to the store manager and we'll work out a schedule for you."

"Great." She bounded to her feet and followed me into the store. I introduced her to Reed, then discussed work schedules and her orientation.

"I have an appointment this afternoon or I'd get you started right away. I'm going out to the accident site with a friend," I told Reed in an aside. "He wanted to see where it happened." I turned to Barbara. "Why don't you come back tomorrow? I'll give you our full introduction to the store. You can officially start work then."

She shook my hand and Reed's enthusiastically then left, promising to be back at ten the next morning.

"That's a relief," I said. "I wasn't sure I'd be able to find anybody to fill in for Rhea. Between the pandemic and the bad economy, there aren't many people free to do a bit of part-time retail clerking."

Reed checked the clock above the counter. "Bad economy for sure. We've only had four customers today. Are you sure you can keep paying Rhea while she's out on disability?"

I waved a hand. "I set money aside for rainy days like this. We're fine." I must have convinced him because he resumed stocking and sorting, checking items off on our inventory list. October and November were always scarce months in the store because tourists had mostly left and the only outsiders who remained were hunters. Most of them knew their way around the woods and didn't need guides. The few parties that did need guides usually relied on people they'd used before.

I went back to the office and spent the next hour on paperwork and administrative chores. It was one o'clock when I heard Reed greet someone in the front.

"I'm here to see Reddy," a male voice said. I closed my file on the computer and stood just as Gideon appeared in the office doorway. He'd changed into a heavy navy hooded sweatshirt over his pale blue dress shirt.

"Am I interrupting, or do you still have time to give me a tour?" he asked.

"I'm happy to get away from office work." I joined him at the door, plucking my jacket from its hook and slipping my phone into an interior pocket. "Reed, I'm taking off. I'll see you tomorrow," I called.

"Sounds good. I'll lock up," he called back.

I led the way out the back door, which Gideon opened for me. "You're lucky to have such dependable people working for you," he commented as we went to my car.

"I know. He and Rhea have been with me through thick and thin. I'm hoping to retire part-time soon and turn the management over to them completely. They know the business as well as I do."

I clicked open the locks on the car and we got in. I backed out of my parking space and headed southwest, driving along Main Street. As I did, I saw Julie's store with a big *Fall Sale Underway* sign in front. I glared at it as I passed.

Gideon intercepted my look. "What? Did I do something wrong?"

"No." I waved at the store on my right. "We're having a sale, too."

He took my hand, giving it a squeeze before releasing it. "Quit worrying about her. You've got a lock on your part of the trade."

"Maybe," I grumbled.

He held up one of the small pamphlets from our store. "This is a great list for first-time hikers," he said.

"You'd be surprised what people forget." I knew the list by heart. Comfortable shoes, good socks, a quality backpack, tent, and a sleeping bag topped the list. It always amazed me that people wanted to take a week-long excursion without the basics.

"I talked to Mr. Hunter today," he said. "I was curious what his group said about what happened to Mindy. He said they were interested in helping. The way he talked, he was turning them loose and they might have some thoughts by mid-week."

"That's good. You might be able to leave before the snow flies." I winked to show I was joking.

"Your grandmother was with him. She insisted on talking with me." His wry expression told me what had transpired.

"Don't tell me. She extolled my virtues and suggested you might want to get to know me better. Right?" I sighed. "Grandmother has been trying to find me a partner since Doug and I broke up. I keep telling her that I'm fine on my own, but she—"

I broke off when I remembered her pungent advice. *A good man is hard to find, and a hard man is definitely good to find.*

"She's from a different generation," I finished lamely.

"Maybe," he said, humor in his voice. "She told me that most of the available men around here were, hmm, how did she phrase it? Oh, yeah. They'd be acceptable breeding stock if the world was ending, but otherwise they'd be so boring they couldn't even entertain a doubt. Or words to that effect."

I laughed. "Yeah, that sounds like her. She's the woman who told me never to let a wishbone grow where a backbone should be. She's got a million pithy sayings for every occasion."

I pointed off to the side when we rounded a curve. "That's where Rhea was injured. She was jogging along the side of the road. Somebody hit her. Threw her almost to the lakeshore." I gestured to Nolan's Lake, which fronted the town on the southern side.

"That's weird," he said, staring at the spot as we

drove by. "How could someone hit her? There's nothing to obscure a runner here." He shrugged. "I still think like a cop, I guess."

"That's what our local police said, too. Jake—he's the Chief—said that it had to be somebody drunk or staring at their phone or something. Distracted driving. That's the only explanation." I pointed ahead. "There are timber roads and other access lanes on this highway, and the forest comes right up to the sides, so it doesn't pay to go fast here."

We drove for another mile or two, Gideon commenting on the dense trees surrounding us. "Lots of logging up here," I said. "The government has strict rules about how much can be harvested and loggers take advantage of every good month they can. The intersection is two hills ahead."

"I'm surprised how hilly it is. I somehow equated lake country with flat land." Gideon stared out his window. "Is that—did I see a moose?"

"Maybe. They usually don't come this close to the road, though. It might have been an elk. Was it grey or brown?"

"It was too quick to tell. Wow. I didn't expect a moose."

I grinned. "If you see one, back away, very slowly and calmly. And never get between a mother and her calf. Moose are pretty laid back if you treat them right. Unlike bears, which can be downright cantankerous and argumentative. They like to prove who's boss." He burst out laughing.

"What?" I demanded.

"The only bear I've ever seen was in a zoo and it was anything but cantankerous. I felt sorry for it."

I grimaced. "I don't care how enlightened a zoo is, it still creeps me out to go to one." I gestured expansively. "I'd rather see critters in their natural place, hopefully at a distance."

I slowed the car. "Okay, the spot is right over this hill. Wulfson came from the left. There's a logging road on the right and it gets busy, so that's why the highway people put in a stop sign. Otherwise, a logging truck can sit at this intersection for a long time, waiting for a chance to make a turn."

"It doesn't feel like a busy road. We've only seen a few cars."

"It's a Sunday and the afternoon. Many folks use this to drive to the bigger town for work during the week."

"How far away is it? How much of a commute?"

"Maybe twenty minutes. Thirty on a bad day. It's twenty-five miles."

He snorted. "In the city it might take an hour."

"And that's why I live here and not there."

I halted at the stop sign, gesturing to my left. That gravel road climbed steeply, ditches dropping off on each side. It was so steep I couldn't see over the top of it, but I knew it dipped, turned, then rose again, leading to a handful of homesteads scattered along the lane. It was like many side roads in this part of the world, roads that snaked around lakes and up hills and around boulders that apparently grew out of the earth like ancient monoliths.

"He ran that stop sign and T-boned us." There were fresh flowers at the makeshift memorial site at the top of the gravel lane. "Somebody set that up after the accident."

I turned and inched along, the pea gravel making the car shift. I hated driving on gravel. It was like driving on ice sometimes and the ditches on either side of this road were unforgiving.

I slowed and angled the car onto the meager edge of the road. That gave us a good view of the weathered white board stuck into the ground, the word *Remember* stenciled on its front. A large bouquet of autumn mums lay on the ground amid the withered remains of other offerings that had been left in the summer.

"Maybe Boyd Wulfson maintains it," Gideon commented, staring at the memorial.

"That asshole? I doubt it. I've never seen who's doing it."

I drove forward to the big dip and the turn where a weathered trail angled back into the dense trees. Hunters used this area and had cut through the underbrush to get to a meadow that we could glimpse ahead through the stunted trees and bushes.

One enterprising shooter had created a modified tree stand which stood about eight feet above the weeds to the right, a wooden structure that would protect the hunter from the elements while waiting for an unsuspecting quarry to pass nearby. Another structure had tumbled to the left of the original one, weathered and worn. It still had a roof and three sides. Maybe it was used by those who didn't want to bother climbing in order to do their killing.

I turned the car around, pointing back the way we came, idling at the side road stop sign.

"The impact pushed us almost off the road. A logging truck was over there." I pointed across the highway. "He got on his CB radio and got help right away. We were lucky we weren't hurt worse than we were."

"And Mrs. Wulfson died?"

"Not right away. She was on life support for a week or so. Wulfson refused to let her go. He insisted she be kept alive."

I leaned my arms on the steering wheel, staring across the highway at the place where we'd been wedged into the car. "Then she had a heart attack and died. I didn't know anything about it at the time. I was in and out of consciousness. Grandmother filled me in later."

I sighed heavily. "I guess it was ugly. When the doctors began taking her body away for donation harvesting Wulfson went crazy. He accused them of deliberately killing her. He threw himself over her body." I shook my head. "Like Grandmother said. Batshit crazy."

"He wasn't injured? Was the daughter hurt? She was in the car?"

"He was thrown out because he wasn't wearing a seat belt. The daughter had some bruising. Woody told me that at Wulfson's hearing, the daughter tried to claim the entire accident was her fault." I eased out onto the highway, heading back to Perrault.

"She was a child, wasn't she? How could she be the cause?"

"She and her father were arguing, and she distracted him. That's what she said, anyway." I gave a disdainful snort. "He'd been drinking so it didn't matter how much he was distracted. He caused the accident."

Gideon turned to peer behind us. "I can see how a distracted driver would plow right through that stop sign. You're lucky you weren't killed."

We drove in silence for a few minutes then I saw a sign for the Shawatok Trail. "Hey. It's a beautiful day. Do you want to take a small hike? There's a great overlook area not far away. It's in a park next to the lake. Not a long hike and it's a good trail."

"Sure. I feel I need to work off that breakfast." He glanced at his feet and his lace-up short boots. "As long as it's not too steep. These are fine on the flat."

"I'd like to work off breakfast, too. And don't worry. There's a bit of an incline at first then it levels off. The view is awesome."

"Lead on."

It took only a minute to get to the trailhead and the small parking lot there. One other car, a beat-up looking pickup truck, was parked. We paused next to the map on a large display board.

I traced a route. "This might be best. The other route is longer and goes through some boggy areas. This whole area is heavily forested." I pulled off my coat and quickly turned it inside-out. "Just in case," I said, slipping it back on. "This is posted land and there shouldn't be any hunters, but I've learned it pays to be careful."

I led the way to the trail which was well-marked with arrows on stakes. As I promised, the well-worn path was steep at the start but within five minutes it leveled out.

"It's nice using one of the state-maintained trails," I said when we could walk abreast on the wider path. "They keep the nasty foliage out of the way. Poison ivy and poison oak can be a problem, but the crews make sure it's nowhere near the paths."

"This is beautiful land," Gideon said, pausing to peer through the dense trees lining each side of the path.

"I've done some hiking in the Bay Area and camping at Yellowstone. I always had the sense of a finite amount of wilderness. But here it seems to stretch forever."

"It kind of does," I agreed. "The Boundary Waters goes to Canada. And the land surrounding it isn't heavily populated, so you do get the feeling you're back in the wilderness, the way it was before man came on the scene. It's different when you're south of here because that's where the mines were. Some areas are totally clear-cut and bare."

We kept walking for a few more minutes, the trail zigzagging through the trees. Then it veered downhill. I raised my hand. "Pretty scenery right ahead."

I took three more steps then we emerged onto the huge rock formation that towered over the lake. Fifty yards below us was the rock-strewn lakefront. Far in the distance was an island.

"That's Picnic Island," I said, gesturing at it. "You can see it from my kitchen window. My house is over there." I pointed to the right. "Once the leaves are off the trees you can see the lights of the house."

Gideon turned, taking in the sweep of the lake. "This is big," he murmured. "I didn't realize how large it was."

"There's actually four lakes kind of hooked together. This is Shawatok. The other lakes extend northeast, like a border around the town."

"The leaves are beautiful. We don't get leaf color like this out in California, not unless you go up to the mountains."

I raised my face, letting the sun warm it. "Spring and fall are pretty spectacular. I love winter, too. There's something about a soft snowfall, a crackling fire, and a warm blanket that's enticing. Summer might be my least favorite time."

"Really?" His eyes were wide and questioning.

"Too many bugs and too many tourists. I don't do well in hot weather. This temp is about perfect. Come on. I'll show you another good overlook."

We clambered along the rocky trail that wound along the lake until we got to a bare spot of ground. From here you could see the town, nestled against the shore and also see how the lake turned with the vast wilderness beyond it.

"That's one of the permit entry points, over there. A forest ranger outpost is there. You can barely see it." I pointed.

Gideon bent over, his head near my arm, staring. "I don't see it."

I bent over, too, my face near his. "Straight ahead then a little bit to the right."

He turned his head and for an instant we were almost nose to nose. Then he straightened slightly and resumed gazing forward. "I see it. That's isolated."

"A ranger job isn't for everyone." I started back, puffing when we navigated the rocky path to get back to the main trail. "I have a friend who's a ranger out in Montana. Now there's an isolated job."

I turned to make sure Gideon was traversing the path okay. The tree next to me suddenly exploded with small, sharp little pieces of bark, startling me so much I stumbled.

Gideon grabbed me and dragged me to the ground at the same instant I heard the gunshot.

Chapter 5

"Holy crap, what was that?" I winced when a rock dug into my side from the trail.

"Rifle," Gideon said. "Are you okay?"

I nodded but stopped when I saw him pull a gun from a holster on his belt and take aim at the trees behind us.

"It was a stupid hunter," I said. "Don't."

"You said this area is a park and it's protected. And it's not firearms season. Why would a hunter be here?" He came to a kneeling position, blocking me with his body. "Stay down. I'll check."

"Whoa, whoa." I tugged him back. "You're not in the big city here. Nobody's taking potshots at us." He hesitated and I could see his indecision. "If we whoop and holler, whoever is out there will get the point."

"A rifle has a long range. Whoever did it might not hear us."

He had a point. I was wearing bright neon green and anybody out in the woods should have recognized it. Before I could stop him, he stood cautiously, keeping one shoulder against a tree while he peered around it. All was quiet.

"Do you see anyone?" I scrambled to my feet and pressed behind him.

"No. But if somebody's dressed in camo I might not see them. The angle of the sun is casting shadows."

He was right again. It was almost three o'clock and the sun was starting its slow descent. "What should we do?"

Gideon holstered his gun. "Find a long stick if you can."

"A long stick?"

He pointed. "That one." While I knelt to grab the broken branch, he shucked off his sweatshirt. He stuck it on the end of the branch and moved it out in front of him where he still hid behind the tree. The sweatshirt dangled about four feet ahead of him.

I held my breath, waiting for the sound of a gunshot. Nothing. He wiggled the branch, making the sweatshirt sway. Still quiet.

"I don't like it," he said softly.

I didn't either, but I wasn't sure what to do.

"Let's try something. Get another stick for your jacket."

I didn't argue. At this point, I'd take any idea he had. I found another branch and slid out of my coat, tucking my phone and small wallet into the back pocket of my jeans. I put my jacket on the end of the branch, which sagged under the weight. The gold sweatshirt I wore was like camo among the fall foliage around us.

"Lead the way," he said. "Keep your jacket ahead of you. I'll be a few steps behind, with my sweatshirt behind me. If anyone sees movement, they should aim for the coats, not us."

"Should?"

"I'm not sure what else to do. We're too far from the trailhead to make a run for it and if we did, somebody might mistake us for wildlife. Walk slow and steady."

Damn. Slow and steady? I longed to run headlong

through the trees, but he was right. Anybody hunting would be searching for random movement within the trees, not someone walking on a path.

I set off, moving quickly in a straight line on the trail. After five or six steps I started to breathe normally and got into a steady pace. My jacket wavered in the air ahead of me. It was heavy on the branch, dangling over the end with the neon bright strips like warning flags in the clear autumn air.

When I could see the parking lot through the trees I stopped. I plucked my jacket from the branch and dropped the stick at the side of the trail.

"We need to report this to the police," I declared.

"Report what? That some hunter mistook us for deer?" Gideon pulled his sweatshirt over his head, his thick silver hair disarranged. I resisted the urge to brush it back into place.

"This is posted land. If we have city people here who can't read signs, they need to do something about it." I was mad as hell and anxious to vent on someone. I figured the police were paid to hear my gripes. "Come on." I stomped to my car, fuming.

Gideon followed, stopping when we emerged from the trees to stare back. He finally got into my car and buckled up.

"Don't tell the police why I'm here," he said while we returned to town.

"What? Why not?" I turned to him, confused.

"Police departments don't like it when another department gets involved in their business. I know I'm not here officially, but it still might create some bad feelings if they think an outsider is here doing a bit of detective work."

That didn't make sense to me, but I decided not to argue about it. I was still pissed off that somebody had taken a shot at us.

"Sure, I'll make up something," I muttered. It wouldn't be the first time I lied to the cops.

I drove through town and made a right turn on Cub Street, going south for three blocks to the police station on the town square. I parked in front and leapt out of my car, striding to the door and flinging it open.

Gideon hurried after me, grabbing my arm and pulling me to a stop. "Relax," he said in a low voice. "Everything's okay."

"It is not okay," I snapped. "Somebody took a potshot at us and—"

"Reddy? Are you all right?"

I wriggled out of Gideon's grasp, almost over-balancing when I turned. Jake Grimly, the Police Chief, was standing near the dispatch desk that served as a counter separating the public from the inner workings of the station. He had his gaze fixed on Gideon, eyeing him like he was assessing whether he'd fit in a cell.

"Hey, Jake." I shook off Gideon's hand and moved into the lobby, Gideon behind me. "Somebody took a potshot at me today out on the Shawatok Trail."

"What?" Jake and the officer with him came forward to join us.

"We were out for a hike. Somebody shot at us." I waved a hand to include Gideon in 'us'.

"I'm sorry. I don't believe we've met." Jake evaluated Jager, reinforcing my notion that Jake was measuring him for a jail cell.

"Oh, yes." I turned to Gideon. Damn. I didn't have a story made up.

"Gideon." Jager extended his hand. "Gideon Jager. I'm in town for a visit." He nudged me. "Reddy and I were friends in college. I was in the area and decided to stop by."

What a good liar, I thought admiringly. That sounded almost believable. Of course, nobody was 'in the area' here. Anybody who showed up here had chosen to come. But maybe it would pass inspection.

"You've stayed in touch all these years?" Jake didn't sound completely suspicious, only a little curious.

"Yes, we have. We were in classes together. Sort of a shared misery, I guess you could say." I tried a laugh and decided it sounded okay.

"Cool. What classes did you share?"

Gideon and I exchanged a look. "Psych courses. You know the kind, the stuff you take to satisfy the core requirements. We participated in one of those extra credit studies." His eyes laughed at me. "I remember how impressed I was with the way you handled the rats for the maze."

I was astonished. How did he know I had to do one of those hands-on experiments and I was the one who always got stuck lifting and carrying the rats? My head bobbed up and down.

"Yeah, the only thing I hated about it was the smell." I wrinkled my nose. "Those labs were so sterile. It always bothered me."

Gideon grinned. "I can see why. You grew up here. It's the opposite of sterile." He regarded Jake with an innocent expression. "We were out for a stroll and a gunshot hit the tree near Reddy."

"Well, it is the season. I suppose a hunter was shooting out of place." Jake sounded unconcerned or maybe unconvinced.

"It's not season," I protested.

"It is for bear," the officer with him said.

I shot the guy a glare. "There aren't a lot of bears that close to the highway."

He grinned. "Tell that to the bears."

I glanced at Gideon. He appeared totally relaxed, hands in the front pocket of his hooded sweatshirt, his gaze sweeping around the small police station. I suppose he was evaluating its capabilities compared to what he was accustomed to seeing.

"That area is posted," I repeated. "Maybe we need better signage."

"Hmm." Jake turned to the officer. "Isn't Marcy out that way right now? Have her swing by, see if anybody's where he shouldn't be."

The officer hesitated and I thought he might protest. "Sure. I'll radio her," he said reluctantly. He moved off, leaning over the dispatch desk to talk to the woman on duty.

"Thanks, Jake. It spooked me." I twitched my jacket. "I was wearing my hunting coat, but somebody still mistook me for a bear. I realize I've put on a bit of weight but that's a stretch, isn't it?"

"Nobody could mistake you for a bear, Reddy." Jake smiled, his dimples a match for Gideon's. Jake was a handsome man, tall and slender with a shock of dark brown hair beginning to show some grey. I remembered him as a gawky basketball player in high school, somewhat shy and awkward. That was decades earlier. Both he and I had matured quite a bit since then.

"Anything else I can help you with?" he asked.

I shook my head. "Nope. I thought we should report

it. We don't have many tourists now, but somebody might get hurt if a hunter is shooting where he shouldn't be."

"It might be one of those city guys who come up for the adventure." Jake studied Gideon as he spoke. "You know how it is."

"Sure do." Gideon smiled, but his blue eyes were as cold as ice.

"Good to meet you, Mr. Jager. How long are you in town for?"

"A few days." Gideon went to the door.

"It was good to see you, Reddy," Jake said in a low voice.

He and I were somewhat isolated from the others. "Good to talk to you, too, Jake." I said it over-jovially, but I wanted to make sure he knew I didn't mean anything serious by it. I liked Jake and that's as far as it went.

I started after Gideon, but Jake put a restraining hand on my arm. "Let me know if you need any help." He studied Gideon, who waited by the door, one hand on the push bar.

"Will do," I said glibly, easing away from him and leaving with Gideon.

We stood on the sidewalk outside the station. "Can I buy you a drink?" Gideon asked. "It's almost cocktail hour."

"Sure, that would be nice." We went back to my car, and I headed for Gil's again, a block or two away from the station.

"I actually did take psych classes," Gideon said. "I wanted to get into the FBI. I hoped it might give me an edge. But then life got in the way and before I knew it, I was too old to apply."

"What's the age cutoff?"

"Thirty-six. They have mandatory retirement at age fifty-seven and I was worried about that." He snorted. "Yeah, look at me now, fifty-five and retired."

"Well, like I said, enjoy it. Not everybody gets a comfortable retirement." I made a right turn on Main Street then a quick left to park behind Gil's. As we walked to the back door, a light snow started to fall, twinkling in the sunlight.

"I didn't think it could snow when the sun was out," Gideon said.

"It happens now and then, usually early in the season like now. It's Mother Nature's reminder that big changes are coming."

We entered the back of the building and wended our way forward to sit at a table near where we sat that morning for breakfast, not far from the bar. The place was busy with patrons watching football games on the television sets positioned over the bar and at strategic spots around the interior. Gil was mixing drinks and two of the regular waitresses were walking among the crowd, bar trays held precariously over heads.

Ozzy Madison sat at the far end of the bar, a beer bottle in front of him. "Hey, Reddy," he called when he spied me.

I waved in reply. Ozzy was an old forty-year-old, his face weathered from the elements and his sparse brown hair standing up in licks, the result of the stocking cap that rested on the bar next to his hand.

One of the waitresses spied us and got our drink order then moved away, picking up empties as she went.

"Embarrass did it again," Ozzy said loudly, nodding

at me. "Thirty degrees last night."

"Better cover those tomatoes," I said. "It's getting serious."

Ozzy turned to talk to another customer. "Embarrass?" Gideon asked.

"A town northwest of here. It's usually the coldest spot in the contiguous United States. They hit thirty last night. Time to cover the tomatoes."

"Hell, at thirty degrees isn't it time to give up on tomatoes?"

"Oh, heck no. We've got another week or so. I've been known to barbeque outside on Super Bowl weekend."

"No," he said in disbelief.

"Sure. Shake off the snow and fire it up."

Ozzy turned back to me. "It was snow, right, Reddy? You saw it." He slapped the bar for emphasis. "I win."

"Win?" Gideon asked.

"We always have a pool on when the first snow will fly." I shook my head at Gil. "I told you this would happen."

He sighed sadly as he mixed our drinks. "It's not measurable snow," he said to Ozzy.

"Nothing in the rules about measurable." Ozzy stabbed a finger at the poster on the wall.

Gideon studied the hand-lettered sign. "He has a point."

"What do you call measurable?" Ozzy demanded. "It's snow. You can see it falling."

"I won the pool last year," I confided to Gideon. "October 7. Three inches of snow."

"Damn. I need to buy a heavier coat. I didn't think I'd need anything that warm this early in the season."

"I'm telling you, Gilbert, I deserve that money." Ozzy pointed at the fishbowl positioned near the cash register, dollar bills almost filling it.

"You heard Gil and me talking about him," I said softly. "Ozzy works for me when he's sober. He's an on-again, off-again kind of drinker. He's on-again now. If I give him a job, he'll be as sober as a judge."

"That's a useful talent."

"I don't have any expeditions booked until next week so he's getting some beer in while he can. I have some leaf peepers coming up for a last outing before the snow flies."

"The snow is flying, Reddy," Ozzy said, hearing my last comment. "You mark my words."

The waitress returned with our drinks, giving me an excuse to ignore Ozzy. We sipped for a few minutes, watching the Sunday night football game which featured the Packers.

"Most Minnesotans have a love-hate relationship with Green Bay," I confided. "It's nice to see a Midwest team do good, but we'd rather it be the local boys. But the poor Vikings are seldom worth watching."

We were nearly done with our drinks when the front door opened. I almost choked on my bourbon. Boyd Wulfson was framed in the entry, his gaze sweeping around the room. He wore a raggedy-looking discolored Army surplus coat and faded, baggy jeans. His black hair stuck out in crazy angles like bedhead. I caught a glimpse of his bloodshot eyes and slack jaw then I ducked my head, scooting my chair around so my back was to the entrance.

"What is it?" Gideon asked.

"I told you, Boyd," Gil called out. "I'm not serving

you. You've had too much to drink already. Go on home."

"I want to buy a six to take with me," Wulfson shouted, his voice loud over the low murmur of the patrons. "Liquor store is closed 'cause it's Sunday—" His gaze landed on our table. "What the fuck are you doing here?"

I winced and didn't reply. Gideon leaned closer. "Is that him?"

"Yeah. If we ignore him, he might leave us alone."

"I need to talk with him." Gideon moved as though to push his chair back, but I put my hand over his on the table.

"Don't. He's drunk as a skunk. It won't go well."

"I can't sell you beer and you know it, Boyd." Gil tossed his towel on the bar top, making for the pass-through near Ozzy. "You're drunk. Go home and sleep it off."

I hazarded a peek behind me. Wulfson was swaying, taking one step forward and pausing like some drunk robot. His gaze was fixed on me, my red hair some kind of beacon drawing him forward.

"You." He almost spat the word. "It's because of you my wife is dead. Because of you my girl is—" He stopped, eyes opening comically wide. "You stay away from us, you hear me? I want nothing to do with you." He towered over me. I smelled his unwashed stink behind me, so sour it gagged me.

Gideon pushed back from the table. "The lady isn't bothering anyone."

"Who the fuck are you? I'm not talking to you. I'm talking to her, the snooty bitch. It's because of her and her family I lost everything that mattered to me. Because of her my wife was murdered by those butchering doctors." He raised one hand, his fist clenched. Gideon came around my chair, ready to intervene.

"You get the hell out of here, Boyd." Ozzy grabbed Wulfson by his collar and tugged him away from me. "You've had too much to drink and you're talking stupid."

Wulfson's arms pinwheeled, and one struck the back of my head. I briefly saw stars. Gideon stepped in, leaning over and protecting me when another fist flailed out. It landed ineffectually on Gideon's back, making Wulfson tip and totter in Ozzy's grasp. Gil joined Ozzy and between the two of them they escorted Wulfson out the front door.

"Are you okay?" Gideon asked, resuming his seat.

"Yeah." I touched my head. "Just a graze."

A few minutes later Gil returned. "Sorry about that, Reddy," he said when he passed our table. "Ozzy's trying to reason with him."

"I doubt that'll work," Gideon said. "He was plenty worked up."

"Thanks for helping," I said. "As you can see, Boyd Wulfson isn't a reasonable person." I sipped my drink, my hand trembling. "If you do manage to talk to him, you'll get an earful about how my family ruined his family. The asshole."

Ozzy came back into the bar bringing a blast of cold air with him. "I tried to take his truck keys, but he got away from me." He shook his head mournfully. "I hate to do it, but we should call the police. He shouldn't be driving."

"I'll do it." Gil went behind the bar and picked up the phone. "I don't want him on the streets."

"I heard his daughter moved back in," Ozzy said. "She came to take care of him. I haven't seen her. I heard somebody at the bait shop say she was back."

"Poor kid," I said. "Didn't she get adopted by some people out in Chicago? Why did she come back here?"

Ozzy shrugged. "Not sure about that."

"She must be crazy," I muttered.

"She'll be a match for her daddy, then." Ozzy went back to his barstool, discussing the fracas with the man next to him.

"It's amazing that he wants to blame you for his troubles." Gideon eyed the door warily as though expecting Wulfson to reappear.

"He's been drunk most of his life. I'm sure it's messed with his brain cells, what few he had to start with. I'm surprised about the daughter. She was thirteen, I think, when she was sent away. I wonder why she came back." I finished my drink and glanced at my watch.

Gideon took the hint. "Thanks for giving me the tour today," he said while we stood and pulled on our outerwear. "I mean it. I appreciate you taking the time to show me around."

"I was glad to do it." I led the way out of the building to my car. The spitting snow had stopped, and night was falling. "I do love it here because it's such an untouched piece of wilderness. I know America has other national parks, but I think ours is special."

He regarded me over the top of my car. "I think it's pretty special, too." Gideon slid into the passenger seat.

Something about his smile gave my heart a little flutter. I drove us back to my store where his rental car was parked.

"Call me if Woody comes up with a lead," I said as

he prepared to get out of my car.

"I don't have your number." I recited it and he tapped it into his phone. Elton John's "Latitude" chimed from my phone, the song I used for unknown callers. "Now you have my number, too," he said. "Thanks again, Reddy. I don't know if I'll find any answers, but I'm enjoying searching for them when I'm with you."

I saved his number then drove home, bemused by my afternoon. It had been a long time since I spent any time with a man in anything remotely resembling a social setting and I had enjoyed myself. Except for the gunshot.

I frowned while I considered that and the memory of how quickly Gideon had pulled his own weapon. I wasn't surprised he had a gun. Minnesota was an open carry and a concealed carry state, and many people had handguns, especially this close to the Boundary Waters. I had a rifle and a pistol at home, and I was trained to use them, but I never carried my S&W unless I was going on a long-range hike.

I pulled into my garage and entered through the back door, my resident feline greeting me with starved meows. I got him placated with some chow then emptied my pockets into the bowl on the counter before going to my office with my phone. I still had a landline because it came with my Internet package, and I seldom used it. But now the unit on my desk had a message light blinking.

I picked up the receiver and tapped in the message code. I heard someone breathing throatily then a murmured voice in the background. I was getting ready to hang up with someone muttered, "I want to kill that bitch." Then the dial tone began.

I stared at the phone in surprise. Wrong number? Prank call? I remembered the doorknob rattling the night before. I went back to the kitchen and double-checked my lock then I wedged a chair under the knob for good measure.

I rummaged in the cupboards and made an impromptu meal out of chips and salsa. I had settled on the couch to channel surf when my cell phone rang. I checked the display. It was Gideon.

"Hello. Did you hear from Woody?"

"Hi, no. I wanted to tell you—I think somebody went through my room."

"What do you mean?"

"Somebody went through my luggage, checking what I brought with me," he said. "They moved my laptop and weren't careful putting things back where they were when I left."

"Maybe it was the maid. Was anything taken?"

"I don't think a maid would open my suitcase and toss around everything inside. Nothing was taken but everything in this room was touched."

"Wow. You should call the police. Or, wait. Check at the front desk. Maybe the management knows—"

"I already did that. They said they had a maid who quit today, and she was the one on duty for my room. Be careful, Reddy." I didn't know what to say and I think Gideon knew that because he hurried on. "I don't know why, but I get the feeling we might have spooked somebody."

I remembered Woody and his trust of a cop's gut feeling. "Okay, yeah. I'm locked in for the night, so I'll be okay."

"Call me if you have any problems, okay? I mean it. I can be there in a few minutes."

I doubted that but I appreciated the offer. "I'll put

you on speed dial," I said.

He laughed softly. "Good. Will you call me tomorrow and let me know how your evening goes? I'm a bit worried about you."

What a nice gesture. "Sure, I'll give you a buzz in the morning. I have new employee training at the store, so I'll get there early to get organized."

"Thanks, I appreciate it. Good night, Reddy."

"Good night, Gideon." I lowered the phone, smiling. I had a guardian angel watching over me. What a nice feeling.

Hoody and I had a quiet evening with no rattling doorknobs to disturb our beauty sleep. Upon waking, I worked out then called Gideon as I was leaving the house in the morning.

"All quiet last night," I said. "I'm getting ready to go to work."

"Thanks for calling. I heard from Woody last night. He wants to meet us for lunch if you're free. He has an update from some of his buddies who are helping with my case. Are you available? He wants us to join him and your grandmother at the CF. That's what he called it. Do you think he knows what that's an abbreviation for among the younger crowd?"

"I'm sure he does. My grandmother was the one who coined the term. They usually dine early. What time should I meet you?"

"Why don't I pick you up? He suggested we get there around eleven-thirty."

"Okay. Pick me up at eleven-twenty."

Gideon laughed. "If this was the city, I'd count on at least a half-hour drive. It's refreshing to not factor traffic jams into my day."

"You should be here on the first day of the fishing opener. It gets pretty busy then. I'll see you in a few hours." I backed out of my garage and drove to town, the sun glinting off the frost on the pavement. It promised to be a nice day, and I hummed along with Pink Floyd on my radio.

I got to the store and spent some time gathering forms and information for our new employee. Reed arrived at nine-thirty and Barb shortly after him. She wore black jeans and a flannel shirt. I had her select three shirts and two sweatshirts which would be her 'uniform' while she worked for us. While she changed Reed and I went over the work schedule for the next week.

I had Barb fill out the requisite information then turned her over to Reed for his own orientation to the store. Several customers came in while they were busy, so I helped the clients who were buying gift packages for Christmas presents for family. I was kept busy until Gideon walked into the store, surprising me when I realized the entire morning had passed. Barb came forward to greet him, but he ignored her and made a beeline for me.

"Reed, Barb, this is a friend of mine, Gideon Jager. He's in town for a few days." I introduced him while I pulled on my jacket. "We're going out for lunch. I'll be back by one so you can get lunch, Reed. That reminds me, I'll be gone on Wednesday. My grandmother and I are taking a day trip to Duluth. Do you think Rhea would like to get out of the house for an hour or so? She can come in and help Barb cover while you're out for lunch."

Reed waved a hand. "If she doesn't want to, I can always bring my lunch."

"I can cover," Barb protested. "It's not that busy."

"We'll talk about it later." I turned to Gideon who had watched this exchange with a curious expression that I couldn't interpret.

When we got to his car, he said, "She's your new employee, right?"

"Yep. I hope she works out. We'll be getting busy in the next few weeks once hunting season opens." I directed him to the Welcome Home Care Facility. "I told you it wouldn't take long to get here. Only one traffic light between the store and here."

We entered through the main door which opened onto the spacious lobby, an area that served double duty as the dining area during mealtimes. Staff was bustling around the dozen white-tableclothed tables, laying out silverware.

Grandmother and Woody were seated on the small settee near the front door. Several other residents were gathered in small groups, waiting for the signal to take their seats. I knew that everyone was assigned a spot which changed on a monthly basis.

"We have the prime spot," Grandmother said as soon as she saw us. "Right smack in the middle of the room so everybody can get a good gander at my guests." She grinned at me and winked.

I sighed. I knew what that meant. The residents were somewhat accustomed to seeing me as one of Grandmother's guests but seeing me with a strange man would surely set the tongues a-wagging. Grandmother would have a stream of gossips visiting her during the afternoon to get the scoop.

"Good lunch today," Woody said with a satisfied sigh. "Jell-o salad, beef stew, and that good crusty bread from the bakery. They do the stew just right, so tender it'll fall apart."

They had to make it tender. The diners would have difficulty eating it otherwise. "Too bad there's not a bottle of good red wine to go with it," I teased.

"I could do that," he said, scooting forward on the seat and reaching for his cane.

"No, you'd better not," Gideon said quickly. "We don't want to share with everybody."

Woody nodded thoughtfully. "Good point. Come on, we may as well get a move on. It takes me awhile to build up a head of steam."

Gideon held out his hand and Woody grasped it, letting Gideon pull him to his feet. I started to do the same for Grandmother, but Gideon beat me to it, leaning over and helping her to stand, tucking her arm over his.

My phone thumped me from my back pocket, and I pulled it out to check the display. *Perrault PD* showed under Jake's picture from my phone's contact list. I hesitated then waved the others forward.

"You go ahead and sit down. I'll be there in a second." I moved back, out of the range of canes and walkers when other diners began to join us.

"Hello?" I said into the phone, turning my back to get some privacy.

"Reddy? It's Jake. I need to talk to you about something as soon as possible."

"Is it about that gunshot yesterday?" I stared through the window at the parking lot and beyond it to the park where we'd picnicked on Saturday.

"No. It's about your friend, Mr. Jager. How well do you know him, Reddy?"

"What? Why do you ask?"

"It's been a few years since you and he were in

J L Wilson

school, right?"

"What are you getting at, Jake?" I turned. Gideon was helping Grandmother to her dining chair. The old woman smiled smugly at her contemporaries.

"Did he tell you about his past? That he was a detective in San Francisco?"

"Yes, he did."

"Did he tell you he was almost charged with murder?"

Chapter 6

"What?" I must have heard wrong.

"Can you come to the station? We need to talk about him. I don't think it's safe for you to be around him."

"I'm having lunch with my grandmother and Woody." I decided it might not be smart to mention that Gideon was included. "I'll come by later. We have a new employee who started today, so I need to be at the store this afternoon. I'll stop after work, around three or four. Is that okay?"

A pause. Then Jake said, "Okay. Be careful, Reddy. There are things about him that you need to know. I'll show you when you come here."

"How did you get the information, Jake?" I glanced at the diners and saw Grandmother gesturing to me and holding up the white dish of orange Jell-o. Apparently the first course had been served. I started walking to the dining area.

"I'll tell you when we talk. Come over as soon as you can." He hung up.

I wended my way through the tables, smiling at people I knew before taking the seat across from Gideon at the four-seater table.

"Problem?" Grandmother asked while I snapped open the napkin and spread it on my lap.

"No, only something I need to do later on." I set my phone on the table, display-side hidden and set it to 'mute'. As the lunch ladies began serving us, I hashed over what Jake had said in between making innocuous conversation with Woody, seated on my right.

I wasn't particularly alarmed. Gideon had said he'd been involved in some nasty police work and perhaps that's what Jake was talking about. It was one thing for someone to be charged and another thing to be convicted. But murder, well, that was serious. I shoved my worries aside and tuned in to the conversation around me.

Woody rubbed his left leg. Gideon noticed. "Problem?" he asked, nodding to the leg.

Woody leaned back. "No. I'm used to it. Happened years ago." He and I shared a look. "Reddy was a youngster, weren't you?"

"Yeah. I was home from college."

"What happened?" Gideon asked politely.

"Bear."

Gideon's mouth sagged open. "Say what?"

"Bear." Woody nodded. "The GDTs were bugging it, and I had to intervene. I don't blame the bear. He was here long before we were."

"GDT?"

"God Damn Tourists," I supplied. "Some idiots thought they could hand feed a bear." I shook my head. "Darwinism at work."

Gideon turned to Woody. "Did you shoot the bear?"

"Hell, no. I just got too close. He swiped me then ran away. Luckily Reddy was with me. She got the tourniquet on and the EMTs were there lickety-split."

I tried to appear nonchalant about my part in that little fiasco. The stupid tourists had milled around, not sure what to do.

"Old Horace is still roaming around these woods," I

said. "Climate change has screwed up their hibernation cycles. It's screwed up everything here. We used to have dogsled outings starting in December. Now we have to wait until January. I suppose that's why Doug called me." I realized too late what I said.

"He's calling? Asking for advice?" Grandmother thumped her cane on the floor so soundly the silverware jittered on the table. "He doesn't deserve to know what you're doing to make up the slack. Don't you talk to him, Reddy."

"Is it a real problem?" Gideon's gaze shifted around the table, landing on me. "Climate change?"

"Yes and no. It means I have to get creative about what kinds of activities I can offer." I sighed. "To be honest, I'm getting tired of pandering to city people who want a taste of adventure. I'm starting to think I need to focus more on education, not entertainment. If we don't change course, there may not be much wilderness to enjoy in the future." I smiled apologetically. "Sorry to be a Debbie Downer."

"No, I understand. It's pristine wilderness. It must be hard to see people come in and trample on it."

The servers appeared at our elbows with plates of food, serving the older people first. When they finished serving Gideon and me, I broached the subject of Woody's cold case cops.

"It was interesting," Woody said as soon as we had some relative privacy. "One of the guys in my group mentioned that when he was on the force, they had a killer who targeted people who got a specific kind of transplant."

I winced. "That's mean. Somebody goes through the pain of getting a transplant only to end up in the crosshairs?"

"I know. We talked about it and a couple of the guys said they'd do some research into any suspicious deaths involving transplants. There are so many variables involved. There's the hospital, the doctor, the organ, the length of wait time." He speared a chunk of potato and let it dangle on his fork. "Age of donor, age of the recipient. They'll split it up and work on it."

Gideon stabbed at his Jell-o, which wiggled in reaction. I wondered if he'd ever had orange gelatin with mandarin oranges. It was a staple in my diet growing up.

"I may be grasping at straws," he said in a low voice. "I'd like to talk to Wulfson but after what I saw yesterday, I'm not sure it's such a good idea. And even if I did catch him when he was sober, what could he tell me? Mindy died two years after her transplant. If there was any problem with Mrs. Wulfson as a donor, they wouldn't have done the operation." He sighed heavily, the picture of discouragement.

"What did you see yesterday?" Grandmother dabbed daintily at her mouth with a napkin.

"Gideon and I went to Gil's for an after-work cocktail and Wulfson came in, stinking drunk as usual." I intercepted her alert expression and knew I'd be in for a grilling later.

"I can go with you if you talk to him," Woody volunteered. "You might not find his place without somebody showing you. It's definitely off the beaten path."

"Are you sure? He might be hostile." Gideon sampled the beef stew. As far as institutional food went, it was pretty good, but it wasn't haute cuisine. He met my gaze across the table with a slight widening of his eyes as though he'd read my mind.

"Oh, he'll be hostile. But he won't talk to a stranger. He might talk if a townie is with you. He knows me. I've thrown him in jail for drunk and disorderly a time or two. Boyd may not like me, but he respects me."

I started to express my doubts but stopped when Gideon said, "Thanks, I would appreciate it. I'd sure hate to get lost in the wilderness."

Grandmother launched into a story about me as a child and one of the times I ran away from home, deciding to live in the forest with Bambi and the other animals. Her tales and Woody's got us through the remainder of the lunch.

I watched Gideon throughout the meal and couldn't reconcile a murder charge with the man I saw laughing and chatting with the two elderly residents. Surely if a man was capable of murder there would be some indication, wouldn't there?

We parted company at the front door, Grandmother toddling back to her apartment and Woody leaving with us. The two men drove me to the store, leaving me there so they could proceed to Boyd Wulfson's place. When I entered Reed took off to go home for lunch, checking with Rhea about coming in for work on Wednesday.

I worked with Barb for the next hour, watching her wait on our few customers. She had learned our inventory quickly and when she had a question, she checked with me. Despite her good performance something in her mannerism felt off to me. It wasn't anything I could put my finger on but was more like a feeling I had, watching her assist people in making decisions. I trusted my instincts around things like that, but until I had more than a gut feeling I wouldn't do anything.

After the customers left, Barb came to my office and rapped on the open door. I looked up from the government forms I was filing.

"I know this might put you in a jam," she said without preamble, "but I have a doctor appointment on Wednesday afternoon. I made the appointment before I interviewed. I can reschedule it, but it took me a few weeks to get in." She rotated her right shoulder. "I hurt my collarbone last summer and it hasn't healed very good."

"When do you need to leave?" There weren't any orthopods in Perrault. Our hospital dealt with more mundane things like accidents, injuries, and illness. Specialized doctors were in one of the larger towns around us.

"I should leave by noon." She seemed concerned, nervously turning a ring on her right hand with her left. It appeared to be a wedding ring, and it slipped easily on her finger, as if it was too large. "I'm sorry. I didn't know I'd be working when I made the appointment."

I knew how hard it was to get time with some of the specialists so I couldn't complain. "We'll talk to Reed. I'm sure it won't be a problem. We can close over lunch hour if we have to."

"Are you sure? I'm sorry. I know I shouldn't ask for time off when I just started here, but like I said, it was hard to get the appointment."

I waved a hand. "Don't worry about it. We'll figure out something." I heard the bell ring over the front door.

"Thanks." Barb wheeled around and left. I heard her polite 'How can I help you?' when she greeted the new customer.

A few minutes later Reed came in the back door and paused at my office. "I talked to Rhea. She'd love to get out of the house. I'll set up a chair for her so she can prop up her broken leg. I told her she'll be like the queen on her throne."

"That's great. Listen, Barb said she needs to be gone Wednesday afternoon. Can you and Rhea cover? I'm not sure what time I'll get back, otherwise I'd come in and help out."

"No worries. I'll pack a lunch for us and if I need to run her back home, I'll close up for a few minutes." He glanced to his left, at the front of the store. "I think she'll work out."

"Good. This was an appointment she made long before she interviewed."

"Not a problem. I'll talk to her, and we'll work out our timing." He continued to the front of the store where I soon heard low voices in conversation.

I breathed a sigh of relief. I had found over the years as a store owner that my biggest problem inevitably came from my employees. Reed and Rhea had been a godsend when they walked into my store, searching for work. I hoped Barb would be as reliable. Yes, she said she wanted seasonal work but that might change. And even if she didn't decide to stay on, maybe she'd be a recurring seasonal employee, who might be as useful.

I continued the usual daily busywork and successfully postponed my departure until three-thirty. I wasn't happy about my upcoming conversation with Jake, but I knew if I didn't show up, he'd hound me until I did. I didn't kid myself that he was keeping an eye on me specifically. He had a proprietary way of keeping an eye on everyone in Perrault. It was one of his good and his bad traits.

I left Reed and Barb to lock up then I drove the few blocks to the station. I was immediately ushered into Jake's office, escorted past an open squad room and what appeared to be a doorway leading to a locker room according to the glimpse I had of the interior. Jake's door was open and the dispatch officer with me waved me inside then left.

Jake looked up from his desk and stood. "Thanks for coming in, Reddy. I think it's better to speak in person." He pointed to the guest chair in front of his desk, and I sat on the hard wooden surface.

"It sounded dramatic, Jake. Gideon told me he worked for the police department in California. He was injured on the job." I figured I'd toss out what I knew and defuse any supposed secrets Jake might think about tossing at me.

"That's part of the story." Jake pulled over his laptop computer and pressed a few keys. "I ran a check on your old friend."

He didn't say it with any particular inflection, but I had the feeling Jake knew how old of a friend Gideon was.

"And why did you do that?" I leaned back in the chair, hands jammed into my coat pockets.

He appeared surprised. "What do you mean?"

"Why did you run a check on someone you just met?"

He gazed steadily at me, but I think he blushed slightly. "A feeling I had."

I pursed my lips. "What did you find?"

"Gideon Jager worked for the SFPD as a detective. He was injured on the job, shot in the leg." Jake recited this in a monotone, his eyes now fixed on his computer screen. "He refused to have a psych evaluation after the injury."

"Psych evaluation?"

"That's standard in any incident that involves a killing. He shot a suspect during an attempted robbery and was shot in turn by the victim's accomplice." Jake's dry, dispassionate voice made this seem like an everyday occurrence. Maybe it was in San Francisco.

"His immediate superior insisted on the evaluation. He said that Jager was showing signs of strain, he was unpredictable and irritable. He was going through a divorce so in all fairness, it might be understandable."

Jake cleared his throat, maybe remembering his own divorce. "Things came to a head when he and his partner went out on a call. They didn't wait for backup and his partner was injured. Jager was reprimanded. A lawsuit was filed. Civilians were injured and they sued the department."

I considered everything he said. There were always two sides to every story. I doubted if things were as cut and dried as Jake made it sound.

"When you called me, you said it had to do with murder. Where does that fit into this?" I tried to keep my voice as cool as his, but I think he heard my skepticism.

"The civilian who was killed was shot with a bullet from Jager's service pistol. The entire incident was investigated, and it generated negative press for the police department. His behavior during the investigation didn't help. He was belligerent and didn't cooperate with the authorities."

"In what way?"

Jake's eyes narrowed. "I'm telling you what his

captain told me. I talked with him at length this morning. The department is still trying to recover from the whole thing."

"Gideon wasn't charged with murder?"

Jake shook his head. "He was assigned desk duty in the Cyber Crimes unit. He did that for a couple of years then he left. From what I was told, it was a good thing he chose to leave when he did. He might have been fired otherwise." He leaned back in the chair, nudging his laptop away from him with a little push, as though shoving away something distasteful.

"Well, that's interesting. I appreciate you doing your due diligence about a stranger in town." I stood, tugging my jacket tighter.

"Reddy, look, your family has been through a lot in the past few years. I want to make sure you don't get involved with—get fooled by somebody who's not what he says he is." Jake stood behind his desk, his chair rolling away on the wooden floor.

"Gideon hasn't told me much about his life in California because it's not something I need to know about. He's only here for a few days, visiting." I managed the lie with what I thought was convincing offhandedness.

"Good. I want you to be on your guard. He may not be the guy you think he is."

"I'll keep that in mind." I forced a polite smile. "Thanks, Jake." I headed for the door.

"I'm trying to watch out for the safety of folks in town."

I turned. "I know you are. Gideon will be gone in a few days, so your worries will be over then."

"Reddy, I—"

I waved a hand. "I'll talk to you later." I beat a retreat, hurrying out of the station to my car where I sat for a moment to calm myself. I couldn't logically fault Jake for gathering information about Gideon, but it still peeved me. Good Lord, couldn't I have a friend and not be the object of speculation?

I drove home and by the time I got there I realized that, no, I couldn't expect that. This was a small town, and everybody knew everybody's business. That's how it was, and it would never change. Nothing to be done about it.

I decided to take advantage of the sunny day and did some yardwork, emptying and putting away flowerpots, mowing through the fallen leaves, and tidying things before winter truly set in. It was getting dark when I came in the house.

Hoody and I had our supper then I started a book on my Kindle and a fire in the fireplace. I was on my first glass of wine when my mobile phone rang. I checked the display. Gideon.

I hesitated before answering, then I remembered he and Woody were going to see Boyd. Curiosity won out. "Hello?"

"Hi, Reddy. How are things tonight? Okay?"

That was nice. He was checking up on me. "Yep, all quiet. Me and the cat are locked in and sitting by the fire."

"That sounds pleasant. More pleasant than my afternoon."

"Boyd?"

"Yeah. Woody and I went out there. He was right. I couldn't have found the place without somebody showing me where it was. It's primitive, that's for sure."

"I've never seen it, but I've heard the stories." I tucked my legs under my worn afghan, sharing it with Hoody.

"Wood-burning stove for heat, a windmill for electric, and Lord knows how many deer hides stretched out on frames. It was a fragrant place, I guess you could say."

"What about running water? And septic?"

"I don't know. We weren't invited inside. I think he had a well. We drove up to the place, but he met us at a gate with a shotgun."

"Oh, crap. I suppose he's got No Trespassing signs everywhere."

Gideon chuckled. "On almost every square inch of the barbed-wire fence attached to that gate. We got the point, especially with a twelve-gauge pointed at us. He did recognize Woody and believe it or not, he recognized me from our encounter in the bar last night."

I sipped my wine, staring into the flames dancing in the grate. "I don't suppose he was anxious to chat."

"You could say that. I barely got out a question or two when he started waving that gun around and telling us to get out. He yelled something about his wife being butchered, cut up for parts, and how she would never have signed anything to let it happen. He said she must have been coerced into signing."

"Jeez, it's not like she was around to care about it," I muttered. "Why not donate?"

"There was no talking to him. Right before we left Woody mentioned something about his daughter, saying how nice it was she was back home and helping him. It was weird. Wulfson got crafty looking, sort of furtive. Then he said, oh, yeah, she's a big help, and he laughed."

Gideon paused. "It was creepy. Woody and I talked about it on the ride back to town. We wondered, well, if something was going on."

It took a second for his implication to soak in. "Oh, God, you mean incest? Abuse? The scary thing is I wouldn't put it past him."

"Woody said he'd talk to the police about it." Gideon paused again. "Better him than me. I don't think your police chief likes me."

"I know he doesn't," I said before thinking it through. Then I wanted to bite my tongue.

"Why? What did he say?" His voice had lost the wry, teasing quality. It was sharper, more insistent.

"He said you had a spot of trouble out in California." I tried to sound dismissive.

A long silence. "I doubt he called it a spot of trouble."

"Jake is kind of protective about our town," I said. "You know how it is. We're a small town and when strangers show up, he worries."

"You get strangers through here during the season. I doubt he worries about them." Before I could reply Gideon said, "I wanted to let you know I've hit a dead end. I think I'll leave town sooner rather than later, which I'm sure will make your friend the police chief happy."

"I'm sorry to hear that. About the dead end, I mean."

"I told Woody I'd stay until he talks to his buddies again. I'm not sure it's worth it but he thinks it might be." Another frosty silence.

"Well, good," I said lamely.

"I'll talk to you later." And he hung up.

"Shit." I stared at my phone then at Hoody. "That didn't go well."

He purred and closed his eyes.

I had another quiet evening with no disturbances. Tuesday dawned bright and sunny, but with a cold breeze out of the north. We had several customers in the store, leaf-peepers from the Twin Cities, mostly older folks who were out for a browse.

I listened to Barb work with a couple of them. She was a tad impatient, but I knew how difficult it could be with seniors, so I didn't say anything.

I ate lunch at my desk and went out for a cup of coffee at the Java Jolt. While I was walking back to the store I saw my archenemy, Julie, walking to her store from Granny's Diner. She and a man were deep in conversation, their backs to me.

She paused on the step up into her storefront and the man opened the door for her. That's when I saw it was Gideon. I almost dropped my cardboard coffee-to-go. They seemed positively chummy, him smiling at something she said. Then they disappeared inside.

Well, that was interesting. I wondered if they had lunch together. And if they did have lunch together, why did they have lunch together? I tried to push my speculation aside, but little niggling thoughts kept popping up throughout the afternoon.

Woody called me that night after supper. "I was wondering if you've talked to Gideon today," he said when I answered the phone.

"No, I haven't. I did see him today. He was with Julie."

"Who?"

"Julie. My ex-husband's ex-wife."

"Oh. That Julie."

I heard my grandmother in the background. "Julie?

What does that little hussy have to do with Gideon?"

"My question exactly," I said to Woody. "I think he and Julie had lunch today."

"He's not answering his phone. That's why I guessed he might be with you." Woody made a funny hmpf noise. "I thought, maybe you and he were, you know, together."

"In bed," my grandmother called out.

"Oh, for heaven's sake. I barely know the man. And I think he's pissed off at me anyway."

"Why would he be angry with you?"

"Oh, Jake did a background check kind of thing and turned up some details about Gideon. I mentioned that to Gideon, and I think it upset him."

"Hmm," Woody mused. "Well, I suppose Jake is jealous and checking on the competition."

I sighed. "No one is jealous of anyone and there isn't anything or anyone to compete for."

"Uh, sure. Okay, well, I wanted to see if you'd heard from him."

"I'll see you tomorrow morning," Grandmother yelled. "I'm looking forward to our trip to the city."

Damn. I forgot about that. I jotted a note to call Reed and make sure everything was set for my day away.

"Tell her I'll be there at nine," I told Woody. "And if I hear from Gideon, I'll tell him to call you."

"Thanks, Reddy." He hung up.

I considered calling Gideon but couldn't concoct a good reason to do so. I tried to read instead, tried to watch television, and finally tried to sleep, but I kept tossing and turning, dreams of Julie, Gideon, and Boyd Wulfson intermingling. I was half-awake at four a.m. when Hoody sat up in bed, growling low in his throat.

The sound pulled me out of a nasty dream that dissipated as soon as I opened my eyes, leaving a residue of fear. Hoody stared at the bedroom doorway and the stairs beyond. Then I heard the noise. Someone was testing the front door, the wood creaking when a person leaned against it.

I leapt out of bed and dragged on sweatpants then a sweater over my sleep T-shirt. I grasped my Louisville Slugger and tiptoed to the top of the steps. Hoody was already there, staring downward.

I put my foot on the top riser but stopped when the door rattled again. Okay, somebody was out there. I beat a retreat and snatched up my landline phone extension from the small table behind me.

I dialed 911 and when the dispatcher came on the line, I gave my address and whispered, "Someone is trying to get into my house. I can hear them at the front door."

"Are you sure it's not the wind? It's fierce tonight."

Now that he said it, I could hear the wind howling off the lake behind me. "No, the front door faces south. It's protected by the house from the wind."

"Okay then, we'll send somebody over right away."

"Thanks." We had a minimal police force in the off-season but stand-by officers were available if needed.

I debated whether to go downstairs or not. I compromised by creeping halfway, crouching on the steps and peering at the lights on either side of the door. When I saw movement outside, I considered rushing and jerking the door open.

Common sense prevailed, even when I saw the doorknob turning futilely and the door shimmy when someone pushed against it.

I waited a minute then crept down another two steps, the darkness surrounding me. We had only two streetlights out here, one near the far end of the lane and one to my right, around a slight curve.

I inched down the steps carefully, my bare feet feeling cautiously along the wood. I went to my left, skirting the entryway closet and sidling up to the window in my den. A dark shape was across the street, running into the trees. The headlights of the police car gave me a glimpse of the figure.

I left the den and went to the foyer, fumbling for a pair of clogs and my long fall coat. I bundled up and pulled open the door when the police officer exited his car, which was parked in my driveway.

I began to step outside, but he held up his hand, shining a flashlight on the front steps. "Hold up there, ma'am," he called, walking in the grass.

I followed the beam of the light and saw what he'd seen. Footprints in the leftover dusting of snow that I hadn't bothered to shovel. The front walk was in the shade of the trees in the front yard and seldom melted until true winter set in and the trees were minus all their leaves. I never bothered to shovel it unless I knew I was getting a delivery or was expecting company. Most friends came to the kitchen door in back.

"I think you did have company," the officer said. He was a large, bulky young man, replete with gear hanging off his belt that jingled as he walked.

"I heard something the other night, too." I reached behind me and turned on the light over the front stoop. "I saw somebody running off that way." I pointed to the heavy growth of trees across the street.

"You keep your doors and windows locked?" He

pushed through the low bushes in front of the den window and tapped on it.

"You bet." I did open the windows in the summer to catch the cross-breeze from the lake, but I had special locks that only let the windows rise six inches or so.

"It's isolated out here." He studied the quiet street, my neighbors barely visible. "I'll see if we can't do a patrol or two this way for the next few nights, in case somebody has the idea they can break in."

"Thanks." I crossed my arms, hugging myself against the chilly air.

"I'll poke around a bit then head out. You don't need to stay out here with me." He swung the flashlight to the side of the house, passing me.

I was happy to escape back inside and close the door behind me. I locked it with the knob and the deadbolt then went into the living room to follow the officer's progress around my house.

He circumnavigated my property for another ten minutes then left, lifting a hand in farewell to me where I stood in the den window. I felt better for his visit but wondered who would be trying to get into my place. I had nothing of value and surely other properties would be easier to breach than mine.

I considered going back to bed but knew I wouldn't sleep so I exercised instead then luxuriated in a long shower. I took my time getting dressed and sat down with a cup of coffee at seven-thirty. I knew Reed was an early riser, so I called him and made sure things were on track for my day away from the store.

"Rhea's looking forward to it," he said. "Barb and I talked about it. I'll come back home and get Rhea at eleven. I'll get her set up and Barb can take off. You enjoy your day in Duluth."

We chatted about the kinds of wares I'd be evaluating before I hung up, my worry about the previous night's visitor evaporating. I puttered around the house then drove to the care facility, arriving a little before nine.

As I expected, Grandmother was waiting for me in the lobby, spiffy in dark slacks and a pretty embroidered sweater set under a bright pink jacket. Her hair was coiffed, and her lipstick matched her jacket.

"You put me to shame," I said when I saw her. "I feel like a poor cousin next to you." I gestured to my dark jeans, rust-colored sweater, and sneakers.

"You're perfect just the way you are. That sweater compliments your hair nicely." She got laboriously to her feet, using her cane to catch her balance, then she looped her arm through mine. "I hope Duluth is ready for us, Reddy. Let's go set the town on its ear. I'm already thinking we should eat at that cute little restaurant out on the lake, the one with the good martinis." She winked broadly at me and waved gaily to the attendants behind the reception desk. "We're off to the city for the day," she called.

"You girls have fun," the lady behind the desk replied.

The overnight wind had calmed, and the sun was bright in the clear blue sky. I guided Grandmother out to my car then paused before getting in. My worries began to vanish with the wind. I slid in and decided to have fun on this little trip.

Little did I know …

Chapter 7

It was a lovely day for a drive. The trees were a riot of color, and the temperature was exactly right, cool but warmed by the sun. We drove along Main Street, and I shot a glare at Julie's store.

Grandmother noticed. "Woody said Gideon and Julie were lunching yesterday."

"I wouldn't know," I said with what I considered to be admirable restraint. "I haven't talked to him lately."

"Hmm. Did you argue?"

"What? No. It's not as though we need to be in constant contact. He's here on business, not pleasure."

"Hmm." Her fingers loosed then tightened on the handle of her cane, tucked next to her left leg. We drove in a silence for a few minutes then she said, "He dropped by to see Woody last night. They had an after-dinner cocktail." She sniffed. "I think he wanted to see if Woody's cronies found anything. They haven't yet."

"Gideon told me he'd be leaving soon." We got to the site of our accident at the intersection where I paused at the stop sign. The flowers from the other day were wilting by the side of the road. I continued on, fumbling my sunglasses on against the sunlight.

"That's not the impression Woody got. He thought Gideon was quite taken with our charming little metropolis."

"I doubt that. We don't have the amenities of a big

116

town like he's used to. No Starbucks, no department stores." I paused, trying to dredge up some other big names. "You know what I mean. Anyway, it's easy for somebody to say they like it but wait until wintertime comes and you get socked in."

"Hmm. There are things to do when one is socked in." She flashed me a smug smile. "If you know what I mean."

I prayed for patience. "Grandmother, quit trying to be a matchmaker. I am fine being single and I have no desire to disrupt my perfectly fine single life by having a man come clopping through it."

She was silent for a few miles. "He's an attractive man. And I think he's attracted to you. At least that's how it sounded."

I didn't want to give her the satisfaction, but curiosity won out. "Why do you say that?"

"Oh, when we were sipping our drinks, he said that he found the town very much to his liking. He'd met so many nice people here. That's what he said." Grandmother nodded sagely.

"Maybe he meant Julie," I pointed out. "If he and she were lunching yesterday, maybe she worked her charm on him."

Grandmother's eyes widened. "That little bitch," she whispered.

I laughed. "I don't think you'll get me married off that easily."

She sighed. "It feels like such a good match. He's single, you're single, he's here, you're here."

"You said the same thing about Jake, remember?" That reminded me of my conversation with our police chief the previous day. "He ran a background check thing

117

on Gideon."

"Jake did?"

"Yeah. Said he had a feeling about Gideon, the stranger in town." I snorted. "What is it with men and their gut-level feelings?"

"Jake's worried that he's got competition. What did he find?" Grandmother tapped my arm impatiently. "Did he dig up any dirt?"

I summarized what Jake had told me. "I can understand why Gideon didn't talk about it," I said. "He has mentioned that he was unhappy during the last few years he worked, so I guess I can see why."

"There are always at least two sides to every story," Grandmother said. "I'd wait to pass judgement until you hear his side."

"I'm not judging him," I protested.

"It sounds like you are. Is that why you and he aren't on speaking terms?"

"I didn't say we weren't on speaking terms. I said that I haven't spoken to him recently. You're looking for trouble where there isn't any."

"Perhaps." She simmered in silence for a few more miles then asked, "Where are we going today? You mentioned something about new equipment. Backpacks? Will you ask me to model one for you to make sure it's appropriate for the lady hikers?"

I recognized an olive branch when I saw it. "Sure. I'll take some pictures, show everybody how easy it is to get ready for a wilderness adventure."

We passed the remainder of the hour-long drive commenting on the scenery, Grandmother's fellow residents at the CF, or the store and the upcoming winter season. When we got to the outskirts of town,

Grandmother asked, "Are you stopping in and visit Doug?"

"No reason to visit. I'm sure he and almost-wife number three are doing okay."

"Isn't it number four?"

I waved a hand. "Who's counting?"

She laughed. We got to the outfitter's showroom, a no-nonsense sort of place not far from Lake Superior. This company served as a clearinghouse for smaller outfitters like my store and we had a reciprocal agreement with them. If I got customers searching for an adventure along the North Shore, I referred them to F.T. Outfitters. If they got people searching for a BWCAW adventure, they referred the people to me or the other smaller outfitters in Perrault.

Grandmother and I spent a pleasant morning examining the new backpacks, which were amazingly lightweight and flexible. I tried on some new hiking boots, expensive but necessary. Grandmother allowed the young clerk to cajole her to one of the display tents that were set up, where Grandmother promptly pulled over a camp chair and directed traffic, much to the delight of the other customers. I tried on a few jackets and pants, modeling them for my elderly critic and we both inspected some of the camp stoves and the selection of dried food.

"Not for me," Grandmother declared. "I like nice fresh fish as much as the next person, but somebody else has to do the catching." That led us to the fishing tackle and into the hunting section where I took pictures with my phone of some of the new offerings. Reed and his brother were my go-to guys for this kind of stock.

We spent an enjoyable two hours at the store, and I

was two hundred dollars poorer when we left. I would have spent more but Grandmother insisted on buying me the new boots and a jacket. We went to the lakeside café for lunch where Grandmother ordered a martini, and I got a glass of wine. We sipped while we studied the menu.

"Soup and salad for me, I think. I love their clam chowder, and we never get it at the CF." Grandmother set the laminated paper to one side.

"Shore lunch for me." I gestured to the window. "We're at the shore."

"That makes sense." She raised her martini glass. "Here's to good times and good men. May we have more of both."

"Hear, hear."

We placed our order with the waitress then we each turned to regard Lake Superior, dashing against the pier below us.

"I never tire of this view," Grandmother murmured. "I do love the forest but there's something about a lake that makes me remember old times."

I saw a wistful expression in her green eyes. "You had some wild times in your youth," I said with a smile.

"Oh, you have no idea." She sipped her drink. "If I have any regrets, it's that I didn't venture outside my comfort zone more often. There were times I could have tried something or someone," and she winked, "but I didn't because I was concerned what others might think or I worried unnecessarily about the future." She arched an eyebrow at me.

I sighed. We were back to that old subject. "I'm not worried about the future. I'm not worried about anything." Well, yes, I was worried that someone tried to break in my house. "I'm not worried about romance," I amended. "I doubt if that is in my future."

"My advice is that you should sample the wares and see if they suit. You can't know what a man's like until he wakes up in your bed after a vigorous night in it. That's when you know if you have a keeper or not."

"I'll take your advice should the opportunity arise."

She winked. "I hope that's not the only thing that rises."

I laughed at her smug countenance and raised my glass in salute.

"Remember, my dear. Age doesn't always bring wisdom. Sometimes it comes alone. And if you can't be a good example, at least be a terrible warning." Grandmother sat back when the waitress set her salad in front of her. "Oh, yummy. Thank you."

I leaned back, glad the conversation had moved on. I seriously doubted a romp with a gentleman was in my future. Like my grandmother, I had a bit of wistful longing at the thought. It would be nice to have someone to share the cold winter evenings with me.

We lingered over lunch. The café wasn't crowded so we didn't feel guilty keeping a table a bit longer than usual. It was after two o'clock when we started the drive home. I could tell Grandmother was tired because she was silent, only commenting occasionally on a sight along the roadside. Well, she was in her nineties, after all, and this was more activity than she had in a normal day. She deserved her little catnap.

We were five miles from home when I realized we were being tailgated. The highway was somewhat busy, but there were ample places to pass, especially because there were special passing lanes on the tallest hills. These were designed to allow a way for logging trucks to be good citizens and let others get around them on the twisting roads.

At the next passing lane, I moved to the right so the pickup truck behind me could get around us. But it moved to the right, too. The grill was large in my rear-view mirror and the windshield was darkened so I had no idea who was behind the wheel.

Other cars passed us on the left. I slowed deliberately but the truck was glued to my rear bumper. It filled my mirror, so I had to rely on my exterior mirror to see the traffic behind me.

The passing lane ended, and I merged quickly back into the left lane, hoping to force the truck to fall back when other traffic came up behind us. But it stuck with me, causing cars behind it to honk angrily.

"Why doesn't he pass?" Grandmother murmured, staring at her side mirror.

"I don't know. He's been stuck with us for the last five miles or so." I don't know why I said 'he'. Probably because I equated asshole pickup truck drivers with the male of the species.

"Pull over. Let everybody pass us." Grandmother gestured ahead to a shabby little bar set off the side of the road, a gravel parking lot in front.

I waited until the last minute then I tugged the wheel, and we jounced into the parking lot, dust raising a cloud around us.

"That was exciting," Grandmother said, twisting on the seat to watch the traffic go past us. Then she turned to regard the dilapidated building near the right front bumper. "As much as I'd enjoy it, I doubt this is the best place to stop for a cocktail."

"I would agree." I waited for a lull in the oncoming traffic, then pulled back onto the highway. We drove another mile, the road winding among trees with a drop-off on the right where we passed above a lake. When we descended the hill, slowing for a logging truck in front of us, the pickup truck pulled out of a side lane and swung into place behind us.

"Damn it, he's back." I slammed my hand on the steering wheel.

"What?" Grandmother peered into the side mirror. "What's his game?"

"I don't know but I don't like it." This was creeping me out. The truck was so close any mistake on my part would send it into my rear bumper and knock us off the road. My hands grew damp with sweat.

"There's nowhere to pass on this road," Grandmother muttered. "Maybe we should get off on the county highway and take that into town. It will bring us in on the south side."

I considered her idea while focusing on driving, a big logging truck with its load ahead of us and the damn pickup truck behind. We were wedged between a rock and a hard place.

"No, that road isn't well traveled. I don't want to be alone on a road with that pickup."

I studied the road ahead. A passing lane was coming up. I followed the logging rig into the right lane and the pickup truck fell in behind me.

We trundled up the hill, the rig laboriously wheezing, tooting, and shaking while it navigated the incline. At the last possible moment, I swung out to the left and passed the rig, leaving the pickup truck behind it. I gunned the car, and we sped along the highway.

"Hold on," I said through clenched teeth. We flew around a curve and there it was, the road I sought. One of the many entrances to the national park was on my left, a narrow lane leading immediately into dense trees.

I swerved onto the road and didn't pause, going far too fast on the narrow track that led into the forest. We were out of sight from the highway within a few seconds.

I slowed and we proceeded more sedately. "What the hell was that about?" I grumbled.

Grandmother shook her head. "I wish we could have gotten a license plate number. You need to report this to the police."

"I'm starting to wonder if somebody's after me. My nighttime visitor and now this."

"What visitor?"

I told her about the officer at my house and the noises I'd heard while continuing our drive. I knew of another exit that would bring us out on the northeast side of town rather than the southwest side where the highway entered the outskirts. It was longer but no pickup truck was behind us, so I decided we were safe.

Safe. What an odd thought. I had always felt safe here in Perrault but now I was skittish. I mentioned it to grandmother.

"It's the unknown," she said with a decisive nod. "Even when you're out camping or hiking you know what might happen. This kind of thing is weird. You need to tell Jake. He's trained to handle weird things."

"You're right." We soon came to the park exit and I entered town on one of the small side roads not far from the CF. I parked in front near the Resident Drop-off sign.

"Promise me you'll call Jake," Grandmother said as I helped her into the building.

"I will. I doubt there's anything he can do. There are a lot of black Ford pickups around here."

"But not that many with tinted windshields," she pointed out. "That's unusual."

"I'll call him." I gave her a peck on the cheek and held the door as she went inside, one hand firmly on her cane and the other holding the door bar. She gave a wave and went to the front desk.

I returned to my car. As I did, I glanced at the far parking lot where we had met Gideon the past weekend and sat at the picnic table.

The black pickup truck was in the parking lot.

I hesitated, not sure what to do. Then I fumbled my mobile phone out of my jacket pocket and raised it to take a picture. The truck started moving but I managed to get several snaps of it when it fishtailed out of the parking lot and tore down the street, nearly hitting a sedan that was ambling along.

I checked the pictures, pinching the screen to zoom in. I caught part of the license plate. Maybe that would be enough. I tucked the phone in my pocket and got into my car. I was almost to the police station when my phone rang.

I pulled over to the side of the street to answer. "I was just about to call you," I said to Jake.

"I read the report about the attempted break-in at your house last night. I wanted to come over and talk to you about it, maybe check your door locks. Would you mind if I did that?"

"I'd welcome it," I said. "And there's something else I want to talk to you about."

"Okay. I get off soon, would that work?"

It was almost four and would be getting dark soon.

"Grandmother and I went to the Duluth for the day. I'll be there in a few minutes."

"I'll be there in an hour or so."

"Thanks, Jake." I hated to admit it, but I was glad to get a second opinion about my doors and windows. The attempted incursions were bugging me. Nothing like that had ever happened before. Why now?

Jake showed up as I was fixing a martini. I figured I deserved it after that harrowing drive home. I ushered him into my living room and lifted my martini glass.

"Are you off duty? Can I get you something?"

"I'm never actually off duty. Thanks for the offer, though." He took the seat across from my couch.

I seated myself, setting my drink on the coffee table. "That's a bummer. Never off duty."

"Oh, I can go off duty now and then. But I need to go back to the station tonight." He regarded me steadily and I was once again struck by how good looking he was. Jake had the kind of wholesome handsomeness that wasn't immediately noticeable but was rather something you saw after you'd been around him a while.

"I appreciate you coming over. I wanted to show you something." I pulled out my phone and prepared to scroll through the pictures.

"Did you consider what I told you about your friend, Gideon Jager?"

"Hmm?"

"What I told you, about his past." Jake leaned forward, the picture of earnestness.

"I haven't had a chance to hear what he had to say. I haven't spoken with him lately."

"He's still in town, though, right?"

"Yes," I said cautiously. "He mentioned he'd be

leaving this weekend, or maybe sooner. I'm not sure what his plans are."

"He came to see you. I'm surprised you don't know what his plans are."

I lowered my phone. "What are you getting at, Jake?"

"Once he got to town, you had problems at your house. Twice. That's what Officer Decker told me you said. I think that's sort of odd."

"It's a coincidence, that's for sure." I kept my voice neutral.

Jake studied me, his deep brown eyes sympathetic. Puppy dog eyes, I thought resentfully. They made me feel guilty. I refused to say anything more.

He finally got to his feet. "Why don't I check those door locks?"

I rose, too, phone clutched in my hand. I led the way through the kitchen, and he examined my back door. I showed him the windows with the special locks, and he approved.

"That works out nice in the summer, I bet," he said as he walked to the den at the front of the house. "You get a nice breeze through here."

"I do." I watched him check the front windows then go to the door, pulling it open. "Listen, Jake, there's something else I wanted to talk to you about." I held up my phone to go through the pictures. "Grandmother and I were followed today on our way home from Duluth."

"What do you mean, you were followed?" He paused in my front door entryway.

I handed him the phone. "That truck dogged us part of the way, out on the highway. I ditched him by going into the park."

Jake studied the images. I peered past him and saw a dark sedan driving past. I didn't recognize it, and I was immediately suspicious given the recent activity at my house.

"Why do you think it was following you?" he asked, handing the phone back to me.

"Because it stayed on my tail for miles and never passed. I pulled over once to let it go by, but it waited for us on one of the side roads and pulled out behind me." I glared at the picture of the pickup truck. "You might be able to get a license number from that."

"Did you see who was driving?"

"Of course not. The windows are too dark. Isn't that illegal?"

"Depends on how dark they are. It's hard to tell from that picture. Maybe it's somebody who was lost. Or maybe somebody out for a drive. Not everybody likes to drive as fast as you, Reddy." He smiled when he said it, but I didn't see any humor in his dark eyes.

I jammed the phone into my back pocket. He was obviously uninterested in my adventure. "Yeah, I suppose. Thanks for dropping by."

"Sometimes things aren't what they seem." He touched my arm. "Call me if you have any problems, okay? I care what happens to you."

I had no idea what to say to that. To my shock, he leaned over and brushed a kiss on my cheek then strode down the front walk to his squad car, parked in the driveway. I watched him go, completely confused.

I returned to my martini and eventually made some popcorn, my penance for overeating at lunchtime. I was in the middle of the evening news when my phone rang. It was Gideon.

"Hi, there," I said around a bite of buttery goodness. "How are you doing?"

"I wanted to drop by earlier today, but I saw you had company."

"I did?" I adjusted the sound, the phone slipping a bit in my hand.

"… more details about my sordid past?" Gideon's voice dripped with bitterness.

"What? You mean Jake? He came over to check the door locks. Somebody tried to—"

"Woody told me that you had a few dates with the local head cop. I wish I'd known that before we reported that gunshot. I'm sure that didn't sit too good with him."

"Wait a minute. What?" I stared at my empty martini glass. Had I made the drink too strong? Nothing was making sense.

"I suppose he thinks I'm horning in on his territory and he won't take anything I say seriously."

"There is no territory." I was talking to empty air. "Well, damn. What was that about?" I eyed my cat as though he had an answer.

He didn't.

I slept poorly that night, tossing and turning whenever I heard a noise outside which was often because the wind kicked up. I exercised in the morning, grumpy and out of sorts at the youthful person on my iPad who kept exhorting me to *dig deeper, you can do it!* I was digging as deep as I wanted, thank you very much.

It was almost eight o'clock before I put that and my shower behind me. I was on my first cup of coffee in the dining room when I heard a car in the drive. I reached the kitchen door as someone knocked.

I peeked through the small window and found

Gideon standing on the back step. I considered ignoring him, but I was in just enough of a bad temper to confront him. I jerked the door open, prepared to give him a piece of my mind.

"I'm sorry," he said before I could speak. He held out a box.

I took it warily. It held one of the marvelous pastries purveyed by the Chocolate Mousse, a café in town. This one was light and fluffy with peach filling and white frosting drizzled on top. "What's this?"

"A peace offering. I've been an asshole, and I wanted to explain." He regarded me with a hopeful expression. The dark shirt he wore under his sweater had its collar turned up slightly against the brisk breeze blowing off the lake. Like the previous days, he wore his sports jacket and dark jeans.

"Come in," I said, standing to one side. "Before you say anything, I want to say something." I closed the door behind him. "I am not dating Jake, and he is a professional. There is no way he'd act or do something because he might be jealous. Which he isn't, I'm sure, because there's no reason to be jealous." That didn't come out the way I wanted but I think Gideon got the point. "Do you want some coffee?"

"Thanks. I would." He scraped his boots on the mat near the door then followed me to the coffeepot. Hoody rose from his spot in the window and came over to give Gideon a good sniff then he wandered away, satisfied he knew this interloper. We went into the dining room, and I divvied up the pastry onto two plates.

"So what's going on?" I asked after taking a bite of the divine confection.

Gideon didn't answer immediately. He stared into

the mug, framing his words. Then he lifted his head to regard me. "I'd like to explain what happened in my old job."

"You don't owe me any explanation."

He cut off my words with a shake of his head. "I do owe you. You need to know who it is who is asking for your help. What were you told?"

I considered what to tell him then figured, hey, why not be honest about it all? What did I have to lose? "Jake said he talked to your boss. You were involved in a shooting and your partner was hurt. Somebody was killed and they sued the police department. It caused some problems."

Gideon kept his eyes on me as I spoke. When I finished, he said, "That's true. As far as it goes. My old boss probably forgot to mention that he was under investigation for sexual harassment at the time and that I was one of the key witnesses against him."

"What?"

"Yeah. Here's what happened. My partner and I were sent to a homicide. We arrived at the scene, and she got a call on her mobile phone. She stepped aside to take it."

"Wait a minute. Your partner was a woman?"

"Yeah. Sarah. Good cop, a twenty-year veteran." He saw my bemused expression. "She was one of the plaintiffs in the harassment case."

"Okay." I could see where this was going.

"She stepped aside to take the call. Somebody in the crowd fired a shot. It hit her. I pulled my weapon to defend her. I saw the guy with the gun. I wounded him. But somebody else in the crowd had a beef with him and the perp was knifed and later died. It was a guess what killed him, my gunshot or the knife."

Gideon saw my astonished face. "This wasn't a nice part of town. I doubt if you've ever seen anything like it here." He waved a hand, encompassing our small town.

"Was she okay? Is she okay? Your partner?"

He nodded. "She left the force, though, and that's a damn shame. There are still hold-outs in the force, people who don't think women belong or if they want to be there, they need to pay, if you know what I mean. Which is bullshit because some of the female cops I know are tough and fair and do the job right. But she left and became a security consultant. She's making more money for less grief. Good for her."

"And your transfer to the Cyber Crime division?"

"I was given shit jobs after Sarah was hurt. My boss made my life miserable. I figured if I moved to the Cyber division, I'd get away from him. But he had friends there and they made my life miserable, too, because I stood up for the women when they brought that suit. I decided to leave."

I nodded. This was all starting to make sense.

"At first I thought I'd find a police job somewhere else, but the more I thought about it, the more I wanted to leave the bullshit politics behind. I'm not sure what I want to do, though, and that's causing me a few sleepless nights." He sipped his coffee then set down the mug. "That's not all that's keeping me awake. This place isn't what I expected. I'm starting to understand why people come here. It's so—so new somehow, so untouched."

"I know. I hate to admit it, but I sympathize with some of the preppers. The back-to-nature freaks." I stole another bite of pastry. "I have to interact with people daily and I'm losing faith in humanity, especially since the pandemic and the Capitol riots and, well, the last few years. It's as though the low life people have surfaced and are getting pushier about what they want. And some of them are coming here."

"What do you think they want?"

"This is pristine wilderness. This is how the world was before humans desecrated it. We should, well, not worship it, but we should respect it, maintain it, nurture it. That's what the preppers and the nature folks do. They try hard to have a minimal impact on the forest. I respect them for that."

"But what about the other ones? You and the Chief—Woody— mentioned the tourists."

I snorted. "Tourists come in and treat it like their own backyard. They litter, they cut saplings, they pollute the waters, they ignore the rules about how to 'leave no footprint'." I enclosed those last words in air quotes. "People don't care about the future. They're about themselves, right now."

"A lot of people feel they've been overlooked or disenfranchised for years. They think this is their chance to show how they feel. They want to be heard. They're afraid of change."

"Life is change." I was tired of the whole argument. "You haven't seen what we've seen. It's hard to explain."

"I was a cop in a big city for thirty years. Believe me. I've seen it." We sipped our coffee in silence for a minute, "This is far more beautiful than I expected it to be."

"I know. It's a surprise, isn't it?"

He put his hand on my arm, his eyes intent on mine. "It's a big surprise. And it is far more beautiful than anything I expected. Beautiful." He leaned forward and our lips met in a kiss.

Chapter 8

I was so surprised I almost didn't respond.

Almost.

It was a sweet, gentle kiss. When it finished, we both leaned back and I swear, he was as surprised as me.

"I wasn't expecting that," I said.

"Me neither. It kind of happened."

I touched his hand where it sat on the table. "I'm glad it did."

"Me, too."

I shook myself out of a daze and took another bite of pastry. "Thanks for telling me about your job. It must have been tough."

He leaned back, his face thoughtful. He had expressive eyes, direct and guileless. Or so I thought. I remembered Jake's warnings, but I chose to put that aside for the time being and simply enjoy the moment.

"For the longest time I blamed my marriage failure on my job. But I later understood that was an easy excuse. I allowed my job to interfere with my marriage. I think Candy and I found each other when we both needed something. Remember I mentioned my grandfather and the family business?"

"Sure."

"He was having trouble around then. The Board of Directors for the company was after me to come back and take over."

"Wow. Could you do it? I mean, did you know how to run things?"

"Yes. A family member has always been on the board, so I was involved. I understood day-to-day operations. But that wasn't what I wanted to do. My grandfather was doubly bitter because I was offered the job and then I turned it down."

"I guess he took it personally." I started in surprise when I heard a knock on the front door then the doorknob rattling. "What is it with my doors?" I muttered, pushing away from the table. "I'm getting tired of people trying to break in."

"Did it happen again?" Gideon swiveled to watch me while I left the dining room.

"Yeah, the other night."

"What?" He scrambled to his feet and followed me through the living room.

"It was on, let's see, it was Tuesday night or Wednesday morning. Wednesday morning, I guess, because it was like four in the morning. Somebody tried to get in the front door." I spoke as I moved to the door in question. "I called the police and an officer came out. That's why Jake was here yesterday. Hey, was that you driving past? I saw a sedan like your rental."

I got to the front door and checked the peep hole. "What the hell does he want?" I jerked open the door.

My ex-husband, Doug Danforth, had his hand raised, ready to knock again. He was a tall man starting to get a bit of a paunch, noticeable in the zipped jacket he wore. Some men should not be allowed to wear tight jeans, and Doug was one of those. He didn't have the physique for it. His once dark hair was liberally tinted with grey, and he needed a trim. Or else he was wearing it longer. His round face was sun or wind burned, with bright patches on his cheekbones.

He looked his age. That surprised me. Then I remembered he was my age, and I wondered fleetingly if I looked my age as well. It didn't matter at the moment. Right now, I had to deal with him.

"What are you doing here?" I demanded.

"I need your help, Becky. My future depends on it."

I winced. I hated his cutesy nickname for me. It always reminded me of Tom Sawyer and Becky Thatcher, characters from books I despised in my youth. "What's the problem?"

He stared past me and did a double take. "Who's that?"

"He's a friend." I half-turned. "Gideon, this is my ex, Doug Danforth. He should be in Duluth getting ready for his wedding."

"That's the problem." Doug pushed past me to stand in the middle of my foyer. "Susan won't marry me if I don't get the problems at the store sorted out."

I closed the door and joined Gideon near the living room doorway. "What kind of problems?" Gideon asked.

Doug gestured to the couch. "Can we sit and talk? In private?" He glared at Gideon.

"We have no secrets," I said airily. "Why aren't you in Duluth getting fitted for a tux?"

"The store didn't fare so well during the pandemic. I'm a bit over-extended on credit. I was wondering if you might consider consolidating the stores again. It helps to have another branch." He dug his hands into his coat pockets like a contrite child. "We had to split up the stores when we got divorced," he explained to Gideon. "It was a big mistake."

"It wasn't a mistake. It was what I deserved. I worked hard to make those stores a success. It's not my fault you can't keep your store solvent. And I refuse to allow my store to be your bail-out. I'm doing fine without you."

"Oh, Becky, come on. I need your help. You've always been there for me."

"What?" I put my hand on my chest. "What? You've called me, what, four or five times in the six years since we got divorced. And each time it was to ask about a business-related issue. You're sadly mistaken if you think I'm there for you."

"But—but—you have to be there. You've always been there." He was truly bewildered. This was the Doug who was confused when I got upset that he'd cheated on me. *It just happened*, he had said in that hapless way of his. *I didn't mean for it to happen.*

I belatedly realized Gideon and I said something very similar moments earlier.

Oops.

"Hey, I get it," Gideon said. "It's a shock when somebody you cared about, somebody who supported you, has moved on. But it's a fact of life. People find other people and life goes on. That's how it is."

Doug stared at him, obviously astonished. "She's moving on with you?"

"Okay, now you're pissing me off." Gideon took a step forward. "Why wouldn't she move on with me?"

"Why are you talking about me as if I'm not in the room?" I put my hand on Gideon's arm. "Let me handle this. Doug, you moved on from me a long time ago. Every decade you get a new wife. Talk to Sally and get her involved."

"Susan. Her name is Susan."

"Susan. She's your new soulmate. We will not consolidate the stores again. Ever. Not as long as I own the Perrault store. Ask Susan to help you figure out your problems."

"Oh, I don't have that kind of a relationship with her," he said doubtfully. "She's not interested in the store. She likes to ski. She has season passes at a couple of the hills."

"Well, there's the first place you can economize. That costs an arm and a leg." I moved toward the door, herding him along with me.

"But I don't know how I can do it."

"You'll figure it out. Without me." I had an inspiration. "Why don't you ask Julie? You're here in town. She's in town. Maybe she can help you. She was involved in the business before you got divorced. You could pay her a consulting fee."

"Julie? I doubt that. She told me she was going into business to try to put me out of business. She was bitter about our divorce." He looked confused. Doug was one of those people who bounced through life, caroming off other people and wondering why they got irritated.

Geez, what did he think? I remembered my own brief Bitter Period, which thankfully was eliminated when the accident happened. Then I had other things to worry about.

"I can't help you, Doug," I said firmly. "Seriously. You need to talk to Susan. You have to include her in your life." Why was I bothering? Doug would do what he would do no matter what advice I gave him.

"I suppose I can ask Outdoor Outfitters if they'd be interested." Doug said it softly, almost like he was talking to himself.

I straightened. OO was one of the other stores in town that managed camping and permits. They carried similar gear as what we carried but they were more geared to singles, either men or women, whereas I frequently had families or couples. If Doug hooked up with them, it might put a dent in my business.

"That doesn't make sense," Gideon said. "You have different clientele."

"Maybe I need to branch out. I guess I wasted my time here. Since I'm in town I may as well talk to them." Doug shot me a haughty look.

Gideon put his arm around my shoulder. It felt natural to slip my arm around his waist. It was the first time Doug had seen me with someone else. He appeared stunned.

"Go." I waved him toward the door. "Talk to OO. I doubt if they'll want to bail you out, but you never know."

Doug glared at me, and I could tell he was searching for a pithy reply. When none was forthcoming, I reached for the doorknob.

Gideon beat me to it, opening the door and smiling amiably at Doug. "Nice to meet you," he said.

"I didn't catch your name," Doug snapped.

"I didn't throw it." Gideon pointed to the front stoop.

Doug hesitated. I thought he might resist then he headed outside, pausing on the front sidewalk. "Apparently somebody else thinks the same as me." He smiled sardonically and strode to his car.

"What does that mean?" Gideon stepped out of the house onto the sidewalk then he turned. "Well, shit."

"What?" I followed him, turning to regard my partially open front door. *Stone cold bitch* was scrawled on the white door in bright red paint. I stared at it, so outraged I stammered. "When did that—who did—why did—" I glared at it, fists knotted on my hips.

Gideon swiped at the paint. "Someone must have done overnight or early this morning. The paint's still tacky. It was cold overnight, so it hasn't fully dried."

Screeching tires behind me made me spin. Doug was racing down my street, one hand upraised to give me the finger.

"Asshole!" I shouted. "I wonder if he did it."

Gideon shook his head. "I doubt he has the guts to do it. No streetlights and only a few houses. I take that back. Almost anybody could do it and get away with it."

"Damn it. I'll have to get the door painted. Oh, wait. I have some paint in the garage. I'll do it tonight when I get home from work." I glared at the door. "Just what I need, another chore to finish."

"I'll do it while you're at work," Gideon offered.

"What? No, you don't have to."

"I know I don't, but I want to. I want to help." He stared at the road. "Your ex is an idiot. An idiot to let you get away."

"I'm glad he did. I can't imagine being married to him anymore. What was I thinking?" I shook my head. "Damn, I sound like Grandmother."

"Show me where the paint supplies are," he said, putting his arm around me again. "I'll get the door painted. You can pay me back by going out to dinner with me tonight. Deal?"

I saw an invitation in his eyes, and I hesitated. Then I thought, why not? Take a chance. "Sure. That's a deal."

He lowered his head, and we shared another kiss, this one a bit more involved than the first one. My heart was hammering when we broke apart.

"I think I got a good deal," he murmured. "Dinner with a beautiful woman for an hour's worth of work."

Beautiful woman? What a sweet talker. "Come on. I'll introduce you to my home workshop, such as it is." We went around the side of the house to the garage, and I tapped in the security code. "Use the same code to close it when you're done," I said, leading the way into the small space.

Twenty minutes later we were back in my kitchen, warmed-up coffee in front of us. Gideon raised his mug to mine. "Here's to getting rid of that pest so quickly."

"Thank you for helping evict him. I appreciate it." It was nice to sit here and relax with him. It was hard to believe we'd known each other for only a few days. It felt longer than that.

Maybe it was because he'd shared the details about his job. Or maybe it was my sympathy for his plight, trying his best to help a distraught mother get closure around her daughter's death. I knew how that felt, in a way. My mother's death was still a strong memory, a pain that was only now starting to ebb.

"I hate to say it, but I need to get going. I was gone yesterday and Rhea got off her sick bed and came in to help. I'd like to swing by their house and thank her." I glanced at the remains of the pastry on the table. "I'll stop by the Mousse and pick something."

Gideon stood and took my mug and his to the kitchen. I followed with the pastry plate. "I'll go back and change into paint clothes then come back and get that door done," he said, leaning against the sink.

Like before, it was natural to brush past him to set the plate down then go into his arms. I had been awkward or unsure of myself during the few romantic encounters I'd had since my divorce. There was none of that here with him.

"I'm already looking forward to tonight," he murmured. Now I was sure I saw invitation in his blue eyes.

This time I had no hesitation. "So am I."

"What time do you want me to pick you up?"

I considered. I had some work that needed doing after hours at the store, budget and personnel things that I liked to do when the store was closed. We closed the front door at four during the winter work week, so I could be done by five.

"Around five-thirty? There aren't many restaurant options in town, but I don't think we'll have any problem getting a table."

"I'll do a bit of research before coming over. Five-thirty it is." He brushed a quick kiss against my lips then released me. We left by the back door, me going to my car in the garage and Gideon to his in front of the house.

I waved when I passed him, buoyed by the morning. Then I remembered Doug and my good mood began to evaporate. I alternated between gloom and glee while I waited in line at the Mousse to buy a treat, then I resolutely pushed my concerns aside while I drove to the Hood house on the east side of town.

It was a sprawling old ranch-style house with light brown siding and pretty red shutters framing the windows. Reed's ancient SUV was absent. He would already be at the store, getting ready to open. He usually arrived early.

I sat in my car and called Rhea's mobile phone. "I'm outside in the driveway with a breakfast snack," I said when she answered. "I wanted to thank you for helping out at the store."

"Come on in," she said. "I'll get to the front door about the same time you do."

I laughed and pocketed my phone while I climbed the three steps up the side of their drive and the next four steps to the front door.

Rhea was right. She opened the door just as I raised my hand to knock. I brandished the pastry box. "It's the least I can do to thank you for helping out yesterday."

"I enjoyed getting out of the house. Come in." She moved to one side, and I inched my way past the cast that adorned her left leg. It encased her limb almost entirely, going from the toe to mid-thigh.

Her doctors wanted her to move around, and she managed well with crutches, but she quickly discovered the challenges of being handicapped. "I have much more appreciation for what disabled people go through," she told me more than once.

Today she had on grey sweatpants, one leg cut off to accommodate the cast and a Visit the Wild T-shirt with a cardigan over it. That was her "at home" outfit. She had a pair of baggy drawstring jeans that she wore whenever she left the house. The pants were loose enough to fit over the cast and were easy to get on and off. I knew because I'd helped her with them.

I came into their living room, a comfortable long rectangle with a big-screen TV at one end, two couches, and two armchairs. Rhea had obviously been lounging on one of the couches because a coffee mug, her computer tablet, and several books were stacked on the long coffee table in front of the couch.

I took the armchair across from her and set the pastry box on the table. "Grandmother and I had a good day in Duluth," I said, unzipping my jacket and leaning back. "You know how she loves those martinis at that café by the lake."

Rhea laughed and sat cautiously with her leg stretched out. She was a tall, lanky woman with plaited dark hair shot through with lighter strands and a long, angular face. "I'm glad you got away for the day. I'm fine to come in and work a bit here and there. The doctor said I can get out of the cast in a few weeks and have a walking one put on. I am so ready for that."

"I can only imagine. Was it busy yesterday? I haven't had a chance to check in with Reed or Barb."

Rhea frowned. "I met her, briefly. She seemed familiar. But when I saw her, she had on a ball cap and sunglasses, so it was hard to tell. We weren't that busy. We had a busload of seniors in mid-afternoon on a leaf tour and they bought some souvenirs."

This was a common occurrence in October in these parts because the fall foliage around the lakes was always spectacular. "I'm glad you were there to manage them. I don't think Barb enjoys working with the seniors."

Rhea picked at the couch cushion with small little jabs. "Reed said she acts a bit impatient with some of the customers. He was surprised she had retail experience. Or maybe she's accustomed to a different kind of customer. We get so many browsers, don't we?" She smiled tentatively.

I nodded, wondering why Reed hadn't mentioned this to me. Of course, we hadn't had a chance to chat in private lately. I made a mental note to do so at the first opportunity.

"Yeah, our real paying customers don't come until spring, usually. That reminds me. Doug came to my house this morning. He wants to combine the stores again."

Rhea sat up, wincing when her leg protested. "What? You're not thinking about doing that, are you?"

"Absolutely not," I assured her. "He wants someone to bail him out. I suggested he talk to Julie."

Rhea burst out laughing. "Oh, that's a good one. She'd probably shoot him."

"I know. Then he threatened to talk to OO, see if they'd be interested."

Rhea frowned. "They won't," she said confidently. "They know he's not a good manager and they won't want to carry him."

"I hope you're right. We have a nice balance right now, although it remains to be seen what effect Julie's business will have on us next year. I'd rather not upset the apple cart."

We chatted about her kids and their sports accomplishments then I stood to leave. "Thanks again, Rhea. I appreciate you stepping in and helping."

"Well, if you ever want to take a longer vacation, you know you can count on us. And if you ever want a business partner, talk to us first." She pulled herself to her feet, using the crutches to do so. "We've talked about what our retirement might be like."

"You have?" I hadn't seriously considered it, but now that she mentioned it, maybe that was a possibility.

"Sure. This is our home, and we love working at the store. If we have a bit more skin in the game, that would be fine." She followed me to the door, holding on to it when I opened it. "We're not getting any younger and we've been thinking about our future."

"I'll keep that in mind," I promised. "Thanks again, Rhea."

"Glad to help." She stayed by the door, watching me get into my car and drive away. I waved and she went back into the house.

I considered her words while I drove to the store. I had never planned too far into the future, but the idea of taking the Hoods on as business partners had appeal. They knew the business inside and out, they were well liked in the community, and I knew they were reliable and hard workers. I decided to seriously mull the idea over this winter.

Reed was sorting through a new shipment when I arrived. A few minutes after I hung up my jacket, Barb came in the back door.

"I hope everything went well at your appointment yesterday," I said when she paused in my doorway.

"Oh, it was okay. I'm not sure I trust the doctor's opinion." She shrugged as though to demonstrate her shoulder's poor range of motion.

"You can always get a second opinion. Sometimes that's a smart thing to do anyway. Although that can be hard here in the north country when we're so limited in options. You might do better to go to the Cities where there are more doctors to choose from."

"I sometimes think medical people tend to jump in where they're not wanted." Her face scrunched, as though she was reviewing an irritating memory. "They can give advice and talk people into doing things they actually don't want to do."

"You don't have to have surgery unless you need it," I said. "I know my doctor now and then has suggested a course of treatment, but I always ask that we do the least invasive option at first, at least to try. Maybe they can recommend physical therapy or something?"

"I wonder if it's a scam," she muttered. "Look at how everything went back and forth during the pandemic. One week they said we didn't need masks then they said we did. The medical people pushed through that vaccine and then look what happened. A lot of people died."

I folded my hands on my desk and considered what to say. By law I was allowed to ask about her vaccination status, but I hadn't even considered it. I knew Reed and Rhea were vaccinated because we discussed it. It hadn't even occurred to me to wonder about Barb.

On the one hand, I doubted if it mattered at this point in the pandemic. But on the other hand, we did get our fair share of seniors in the store and many of them were fragile.

"The amount of people who died were a small fraction of those who were vaccinated," I said reasonably. "There are always risks with medical advancements."

Barb appeared skeptical. "I suppose you're right," she said grudgingly. "But sometimes I think they use us as guinea pigs or something."

I was hard-pressed to believe anyone could coerce her. "I'm sure they have your best interests at heart," I said lamely.

"I doubt that." She moved on into the store and I heard her greeting Reed.

I returned to my perusal of canoe catalogs, wincing

when I saw the prices. We rented most of our more expensive items and canoes were right up there. The newer ones were nice, and I worked on my budget most of the morning, figuring a way to afford a couple of new ones to add to our aging inventory.

The morning passed and Barb left for lunch. I came out of my office to the front where Reed was finishing with a customer.

"I stopped to see Rhea," I said when we were alone. "She's getting around pretty good with those crutches."

"I'll be glad when she's back to a hundred percent. I never knew how hard it was to haul laundry up those basement steps. I may need to consider changing that if we want to stay in that house when we retire." He turned to face me, his plain face thoughtful. "I wanted to mention something and maybe it's not my business, but I think I should tell you."

He sounded serious. I leaned on the counter. "Go ahead."

"It's about Barb."

I waved a hand. "Rhea mentioned that she gets impatient with customers sometime."

"Yeah, there's that. It's hard to say how she'll be in the spring, when we get busy. I get the feeling she's more accustomed to working with a younger crowd, people who are true outsiders, not the kind of newbies we get at this time of year."

"That's possible," I said. "I was only able to verify the dates of her employment at the store in the Twin Cities. By law they can't tell me much of anything about how she worked."

Reed leaned on the checkout counter. "I'm willing to give her the benefit of the doubt about that. The thing that bugs me, though, is she's been asking questions about you and your grandmother. She wanted to know about the accident and your mother's death. I don't know, it's like every day she's asking for more details about you."

"That's odd," I agreed. "She did tell me that she respected the fact that I was a woman in what was normally a man's line of work. Maybe she wants to take a similar path."

He shook his head. "No, it doesn't feel like that. It feels more personal than that. Maybe she's curious because you're the boss." He sounded doubtful.

"Thanks for telling me," I said. "I'm sure it's general curiosity. Listen, I wanted to warn you. Doug showed up at my house, asking if we'd combine the stores again."

Reed's reaction was as forceful as Rhea's. "What? Why would you do that? We're doing fine without him. You told him that, right?"

"I sure did." I summarized what Doug had said about approaching our competitor.

"That could cause problems if they joined forces," he mused. "I'll ask around and see if I can scope out any information."

"Thanks, Reed." I knew he had his friends in town who would keep him apprised of any changes at the competition. It was useful to have somebody on staff who was such a mainstay in our small community. "I'm going out for coffee. I'll be back soon."

"I'll go out for lunch when Barb gets back. Take your time."

I went next door to the Java Jolt and got my early afternoon fix. As I did, I glimpsed the café a few doors away where I'd seen Julie and Gideon the other day. I remembered that I hadn't asked him about his lunch with her.

Well, how could I as him? 'Hey, I saw you with my biggest rival and wondered what you were talking about?' That wouldn't be too cool. I mulled over how to work it into conversation when I saw him that night.

The night. Hmm. What would happen tonight? Well, dinner, for one thing. I would try to wrap up here early so I could go home and have time to decide what to wear. Perrault didn't have any haute dining spots, but the few restaurants we did have merited better than a sweatshirt and jeans. It was a pleasant thought.

We had a quiet afternoon with only a few customers, two of whom were interested in camping gear and entry permits. I listened with half-attention while Barb and Reed worked with the men and what I could hear sounded okay. Maybe she had problems with the older set. Heaven knew they could be challenging.

Reed and Barb left shortly after four o'clock, Reed locking the front door and flipping the Open/Closed sign. I heard Reed lock the back door behind him then the store fell quiet. I focused on my tasks, working out next year's budget, a chore I hated but knew was essential. I wrapped up a first draft in forty-five minutes or so and stood, ready to pull on my jacket.

Someone rattled the front door. I got up from the desk and peeked around the doorframe. Our "Closed" sign was in place. I couldn't see clearly who was outside. A reflection on the glass of the door effectively hid the person.

I turned back to my desk, but the rattling came again. I was getting ready to call out 'We're closed' when my desk phone rang. It was a simplified business model with a square display and buttons for voice mail, speaker, speed dialing, and volume control next to the cordless receiver.

I checked the large display at the caller ID on the screen. *Unknown number.* The phone rang and the door rattled again, louder this time. Was someone trying to break in? Good Lord, we had a storefront on Main Street. Who would be that stupid?

The phone rang for the third time then switched to our phone message. "We're closed right now and will open tomorrow morning. If you need to contact us after hours, please leave a message."

Any voice mail would be forwarded immediately to my home phone and my cellphone, a precaution we took in case one of our outfitter reservations had to cancel or had last-minute worries. We'd learned the hard way to always be in touch with customers.

"You stone cold bitch." The voice was harsh and raspy, so guttural I could barely understand the words. "You're gonna die soon."

Chapter 9

I froze, my hand hovering over the phone. The caller had hung up.

The doorknob rattled again. I jerked so badly I knocked into the phone with my elbow. "Son of a bitch," I hissed.

I lunged for the base unit, but it clattered off the desk, dangling inches above the wooden floor by its cord which snaked into the wall socket. The portable receiver, unfettered by a cord, bounced away and skittered under my desk.

I stood there, uncertain which way to turn. I peeked out the door again, but it was silent at the front of the store. Had the person left? I thought about sidling out and peering through the window, but the light from my office would highlight me in the dark storefront. Was it safe?

Holy crap, why was I thinking that? I was often here alone at night and never once had I worried about it. Now I was jumping at shadows. Okay, get a grip.

I dropped to my knees and crawled on the floor, rescuing the phone from the dust bunnies under my desk. I had a cleaning lady come in on Tuesday and Friday and I made a mental note to talk to her when she came in tomorrow evening.

I wiped the phone on my jeans and dropped it back in its base. The place was abnormally quiet now. I found myself tiptoeing around my desk to shut off my computer and turn off the light.

I stood, the only light coming from the cell phone clutched in my hand. I listened intently but heard no indication anyone was outside the front door. I peeked around the doorframe and did not see a shadow or any movement.

I fumbled for and found my jacket and pulled it on. Then I tiptoed along the hallway to the back door. I listened against it but heard nothing. I jammed my phone into my pocket and threw open the door, hoping to startle any would-be trespassers.

No one there. Thank heavens. I might have had heart failure if someone was. I pulled the door shut behind me, tested the automatic lock by jiggling the door, and ran to my car, all in about ten seconds. I relaxed when I was inside.

My nerves steadied on the drive to my house, and I was able to review things a bit more pragmatically. Someone was playing serious pranks on me, but who? As far as I knew I had never offended anyone so dramatically that they'd try to break in my home or threaten me. I mentally sorted through customers, contacts, and townspeople but honestly couldn't find anyone that might have it in for me.

When I got to the house I slowed to study the front door. It appeared brand new, the white paint shiny in the darkening day. I pulled in my drive and paused to wait for the garage door to open. As I did a car pulled in behind me.

I had a brief instant of panic until I saw Gideon in the driver seat. Damn. I was running late. I parked in the garage and came out to meet him as he got out of his car. He wore the tweed jacket with black dress pants and a dark sweater, an outfit that was stylish but casual.

"Sorry, I'm late," I said.

He grinned. "I'm early. No rush. I made a reservation for us at The Den for six, so we have plenty of time. It's only five-fifteen."

I led the way to the back door. "Your paint job is great. I hope it wasn't too much of a hassle to do it."

"I didn't mind at all." We entered the kitchen. I saw the blinking message light on my landline phone and unthinkingly pressed the button to play the message.

The harsh, guttural voice echoed in my quiet kitchen, repeating the earlier threat.

"What the hell?" Gideon reached for the machine then stopped. "When did you get that?"

"It came in at the store a few minutes ago. The voice mail gets forwarded here and to my phone." I pulled my mobile out of my back pocket and brandished it. "I was there after hours working on some stuff. Somebody kept trying the doorknob, too."

Gideon stared at the phone then me. "As much as I hate to say it, we need to tell the police about this. And show them this." He pulled out his phone and thumbed through the icons, holding it up so I could see my defaced front door. "In case we need evidence."

"I never thought about it," I admitted. "We can stop on our way to the restaurant. It won't take me long to get ready. Could you top up Hoody's food bowl? The kibble is in that cupboard." I pointed to the white cupboard near the fridge.

"I've got it."

I pulled him to me and kissed him quickly. "I like having help around the house. Thanks."

"My pleasure." His eyes laughed with mischief.

I hurried upstairs and changed into black slacks and my prettiest sweater, the one with the high collar and a big red snowflake on a grey background. The color exactly matched my hair, which I held away from my face with one large crystal snowflake barrette. Snowdrop earrings completed my fashion statement. I spent a few minutes with face powder, eye shadow and mascara and I was ready to go.

"You weren't kidding when you said it wouldn't take long to get ready," Gideon said when I rejoined him in the kitchen.

"I'm low maintenance." I went to the coat closet near the door and slipped on my low-heeled black boots to round out my ensemble. I plucked a small black purse from its hook and tucked in my mobile phone and keys, then pulled out a dark red wool cape and handed it to Gideon. He settled it around me.

It was a short drive to the police station. I was relieved to see that Jake wasn't anywhere in sight. The woman on duty at the desk took the details about the phone call, listened to the copy I had on my mobile phone, then studied the pictures Gideon showed her.

"It's probably a prank," I said. "An officer came to the house the other night because I heard an intruder trying to get in the door. Maybe it's more of the same."

The woman checked my address. "Oh, yeah. We've been doing spot checks out that way for the last day. I'll let the Chief know and see how he wants to proceed."

I started to protest but stopped when Gideon took my hand and gave it a gentle squeeze. "He knows how to contact us if he has questions," he said.

We left, pausing in the front doorway so I could adjust my cape. Jake had emerged from the back and was leaning over the woman, looking at what she'd written. He looked up and saw me then his gaze shifted to Gideon, who was holding the door. It was obvious from the way we were dressed we were going out together. Jake's eyes narrowed then his eyes moved back to me. I saw disappointment and anger there.

I hurried away, not anxious for a confrontation. "I think it's time for a cocktail," I said when Gideon opened the car door for me.

"That sounds like the perfect start to a perfect evening." He closed the door. As he walked around the rear of the car, I saw Jake watching us from the door of the police station.

Gideon saw him, too. He gave a jaunty wave then got into the driver's seat. "Let the police worry about your problems," he said. "Let's have fun tonight."

"I like the way you think."

We got to The Den, an elegant restaurant perched on a rocky overlook near the lake. It was one of three high-end dining spots in the area and was the only one that opened solely for dinner. The others catered to the lunch crowd as well. The Den had several dining rooms strung together like jewels along the shore, the lights reflecting into the water.

We were led to a two-person table in the center section, walking through two rooms to get there. The long bar was off the first room, a semi-circular affair that easily sat twenty people with plenty of room to spare. I glimpsed a familiar face or two, but it was hard to tell for sure in the low light.

A waiter appeared and we ordered cocktails: a martini for me and a bourbon on the rocks for Gideon. While we waited for our libations, we studied the menu.

I was a sucker for a good steak, so it was easy for me.

I stared out the window at the lake and saw a reflection behind me. "Oh, great. Just what I need. A confrontation with my ex-husband's ex-wife."

"What?"

"We're being paid a visit." I plastered a fake smile on my face. "Hey, Julie."

Doug's ex came to a stop next to our table. Julie was still slender, still tall, and still had honey blonde hair done up in a messy bun that threatened to tumble at the least provocation. I did some fast math. She was thirty now, I think, and I could see small signs of aging around her eyes and mouth. I saw that her skin was also starting to lose that amazing elasticity of youth.

Of course, she'd recently gone through a messy divorce and that could age anyone. She wore dark leggings and a body-hugging knit top that came to mid-thigh, subtly emphasizing her figure without shouting it. That was a change from her former appearance, which had been Blatant Sex Kitten.

She glanced at Gideon then kept her attention on me. "I was wondering if I could talk with you about a business proposition."

I leaned back, wariness kicking in. "First Doug, now you. What is the world coming to?"

"Did he finally approach you? I wondered if he would do it sooner rather than later." She rolled her eyes as though to tell me *what an idiot*.

"You knew?"

Her blonde bun wobbled precariously when she nodded. "He told me he was talking to you first, but he knew you'd turn him down. He wanted to make it look good, though."

"Then he could go to your competitor and not seem like a bad guy." Gideon sipped his drink. "Smart."

"That rat," I muttered. "He still has friends, contacts in town. I suppose he didn't want to shred his reputation."

"Doug doesn't want to work. I loved being in the store, but he hated it." She saw the menus on our table. "I don't want to interrupt your dinner. Could we talk after you've dined? Ron and I are starting our salad course. Could we wait for you in the bar? I have something to discuss with you."

I started to wave her away then reconsidered. It wouldn't hurt to talk to her. After all, she was a competitor of sorts. Maybe I could get some inside scoop on how she was doing.

I looked at Gideon. "Would that be okay with you?"

"Sure. We can have our after-dinner drink in the bar with your friends." He smiled politely at Julie.

"Thanks. I appreciate it. I'll talk with you later." Julie beamed at us then flounced away, causing a few male heads to turn in her direction.

"What does she want?" I wondered out loud. "And I guess you were right." I peered past the diners and saw Julie join Ron Hood at a table in the next room. Ron saw me and gave a little wave then stood to pull out Julie's chair for her.

"Right about what?" Gideon sipped his bourbon.

"She's with Ron Hood. Maybe it is romance and not poaching. Or maybe she's trying to talk him into working for her." I scowled then took a calming sip of my drink. The gin did the trick, and my pulse steadied. "Well, we'll find out soon enough."

"I like the way you do that. You partition off your

worries and deal with them later. You don't let them interfere with the moment. I need to learn to do that. I seem to keep my worries always churning in the back of my mind."

"You appear to be totally relaxed."

"Little do you know." His blue eyes watched me over the rim of the heavy tumbler in his hand. I shivered at the expression I saw there.

The waiter came and we placed our orders. "Tell me something about your life as a detective," I prompted when we were alone again. "Is it like on television? I know you don't catch the bad guys in forty-five minutes, but there must be some exciting moments."

Small dimples flashed at the corner of his mouth. "I suppose you could say that. My partner and I had some tough cases. I think the hardest one was a woman who killed anyone who she saw as a competitor."

I thought of Julie. "What kind of competitor?"

"This woman had a beauty salon and apparently had some cutting-edge stylists working for her. No pun intended," he added with a wink. "When one of the stylists turned up missing, the stylist's husband filed a report. We started at the salon when we found out another stylist had left but she didn't have any family in town to report her missing."

"What happened?"

"The salon owner was so upset that her people were leaving she killed them. In kind of a grisly way. I don't think I want to talk about it before we eat."

I shuddered. "I can't imagine killing anyone. It's so…final somehow."

"It is that. It's been my experience that women usually prefer long-distance murder." He sipped his bourbon, acting like it was the most natural opinion in the world.

"Say what?"

"They tend to use poison. They don't get close when they kill. A man will aim a gun at someone and pull the trigger. A woman has trouble doing it."

I considered that. "I guess it depends on what their motive is. Do they want to inflict pain or fear? Do they want to see the person die?" I shuddered. "Gruesome talk."

"Let's change the subject. What do you think the ex-wife wants to discuss?" His eyes went past me to where I know Julie and Ron were seated.

"I have no idea."

"I do," he said with a sly expression.

"You do? Why?" I leveled a finger at him. "Does this have to do with the lunch you had with her?"

He laughed. "This town! Can't a guy have lunch with somebody without somebody reporting on him?"

"Nope. Small town, big gossips. Come on, tell me."

"All I'll say is that she and I talked about a business idea she had. I think it has merit. I hope you'll let her give her pitch."

The waiter appeared with our salads and somehow Gideon turned the conversation away from Julie and onto a discussion of our dogsled outings, scheduled to begin in January. He peppered me with questions about how it was run, where we lodged people, and he was especially curious about our camping trips.

"I can't believe it," he said while we dug into our meals. "People actually pay to camp outside, in the wintertime, in a remote setting with campfires, tents, and dogs doing the legwork."

"Oh, there's plenty of legwork for humans." I remembered the cross-country skis, the snowshoes, and the packs that we had to haul to make sure the experience was safe and comfortable.

I worked with an expert group who managed most of the actual details of the trip. Our store mainly dealt with booking the reservations and helping people get outfitted so they didn't freeze to death.

"I might go out with the late January group," I said. "I like to do one camping trip a year. The other dogsled trips work out of one of the lodges in the B-dub."

"That sounds more like it," he said. "A chance to do a bit of snow work during the day then a nice, warm room at night with a hot meal waiting."

"It is nice," I admitted. "The camping trips are a ton of work for everybody involved. Fun, but work. The lodge trips are easier."

"I may have to try one of those," he said, pushing away his plate and leaning back. "Maybe in January." He rubbed his hands together. "Or maybe I should wait until spring and come back for some fishing."

"Or do both," I suggested. I surveyed the remains of my meal, happy that I would have leftovers to take with me. That steak was fabulous and would be equally fabulous on a steak salad tomorrow.

"Maybe both," he agreed.

We lingered over coffee then I sighed. "Let's get this over with," I said, pushing back my chair. I had already paid the bill at my insistence to repay Gideon for his help with the front door. He also insisted on buying me a drink in the bar after dinner.

Gideon came around the table and held out his arm. "That's the attitude."

I shot him a glare. "Okay, so I'm a bit suspicious. Don't forget, this woman stole my husband away from me."

"And if she hadn't, you wouldn't be here with me tonight." He said this leaning close to me and whispering in my ear. I shivered at his nearness.

We went into the bar. I saw Julie immediately, seated at a low table to my left. Ron was at the bar, a glass of beer in front of him. I approached Julie and she stood.

"I know you have every reason to hate me," she began.

I held up a hand. "Trust me. I don't hate you. At first I resented you, but later I came to understand you did me a favor."

"Well, I do need to apologize for that day at the gym."

I saw the sharpened interest in Gideon's blue eyes when he remembered my comment about an unpleasantness at a gym. I would have some explaining to do later.

I waved a hand. "No, nothing to apologize for." I sat, my back to the bar and the people there. Gideon sat next to me.

She resumed her seat. "No, I need to apologize. I was young and stupid when I said those things. I never thought anything would change." I saw the hurt in her eyes. "I didn't know what it was like to get older," she finished in a rush.

"You're only thirty, Julie. You're not over the hill." I considered my words. "Hell, there isn't even a hill anymore. A woman can be whoever she wants to be at whatever age she is. Don't let anybody tell you otherwise."

"Bravo," Gideon whispered.

"I know. But it's still different. I do want to apologize. And I want to talk to you about a business proposition whenever you have the time." She glanced at Gideon. "In private, if that's okay."

Gideon stood. "No time like the present. I'll join Ron at the bar. What can I get you?" He leaned over me, smiling.

"Brandy would be nice."

"Two brandies, coming up." He sauntered away.

"He's nice," Julie said. "Are you and he…?"

"No, nothing like that." I chewed on my lower lip thoughtfully. Hmm. I kind of liked that idea. "What did you want to talk about?"

Julie stared into her wine glass then up at me. "I think I'm in over my head with my store," she said without preamble. "I want to propose a partnership of sorts."

I regarded her warily. "What kind of partnership?"

"You know about setting up trips, the entry permits and the gear and the locations based on the skill level of the people going."

She was right. My shop was known for customizing outings depending on the customer. It wouldn't do to set up a mile-long portage for someone who could barely lift a canoe. A "lightweight camping package" could accommodate a minimal lack of physical ability but not a complete lack.

"Yeah, I've been doing it for years," I said. "My clerks know how to interview clients to get the right mix of gear and trails. We developed a great survey we send to people, and they fill it out ahead of time. Then we come up with an itinerary that we can tweak when we actually meet the campers and find they've over-estimated their abilities."

"Exactly." Julie pounced on this so quickly I knew it must have been a problem for her. "You're all about the physical side of it. I'm about the retail side of it. I mean, you do have retail goods but most of it is so utilitarian. I've found that people like to get something that commemorates this experience." She raised her hands as though the cozy bar was the forest. "City people eat that up. They want to have a nice, tangible souvenir of their adventure."

She had a point. Most of the gear we sold was tough, durable, and, well, yes, utilitarian. We had nothing that anyone would want to parade around a high-tone suburb to show off their camping experience. Let's face it, a canvas jacket would be out of place in the Mall of America whereas a pretty down jacket with faux fur collar would be right at home. Cute hiking boots? Maybe, as long as they weren't seasoned with moose poop or water stains.

"I never thought of it that way," I admitted. "What were you thinking about?"

"I send people your way when they want to plan their outings. You can send people my way when they find they need to buy the right kind of clothing. I could even take over that part of your store and stock it and maintain it. That way I can specialize in clothing and you can focus on expeditions."

I considered the idea. I had a paltry selection of retail clothing more for those people who forget to bring the right socks or gloves or hats. I didn't have a large inventory of pants, shoes, shirts, and jackets. It was all I could do to keep up with the technical improvements to ropes, canoes, camping supplies, and maps. Clothing was always being tweaked for weight, weather, and fit but I didn't keep up with style. I was the first to admit I wasn't well-versed in the niceties of woodland fashion.

If I didn't have to worry so much about retail, maybe I could add some of the new trip packages my guides and I had discussed over the summer. A couple of the guys wanted to go further inland for longer trips. I wanted to try the route myself so I could properly assess it for customers. If Julie would handle the merchandise part of the store, I could take time away and Reed could handle everything else.

"That might work," I said slowly. "It would let me concentrate on the stuff I enjoy doing."

"Exactly," she said. "We could combine my retail experience with your camping experience and come up with some glamping outings. Sort of take things to the next level."

"Glamping?" I asked doubtfully. "What do you mean?"

"Okay, see." She whipped out one of my brochures that described a week-long excursion. "What if you have guides meet people at the different stopping points and the tents are already set up? The food has been packed in for them and they only have to relax, fix a drink, and enjoy it?"

"I don't know. Most of the people I work with are anxious for the whole nature experience. I mean, that's what's so cool about the Boundary Waters. You can go for days and never see another person."

"What about on the last night of their trip? Or maybe after a hard part of the hike? Wouldn't it be nice to relax and not have to think about setting up a camp site? You're doing something similar for the dogsled trips. Why not do it for the fishing and hiking trips?"

She had a point, I had to admit. For first-timer campers, it could be a bit rough sometimes, especially if they had bad weather or a tough trail. It was tempting.

"You handle the gear and the trips. I handle the clothing and the memories."

"Memories?" I asked.

"Camera and video equipment that they can rent and take with them. They don't have to risk their phones."

"Phone locker rental." Gideon resumed his seat next to me, setting two glasses of brandy on the table. "They leave their tech here and borrow somebody else's."

"You guys discussed this," I accused.

Gideon gave me a meek look. "I told her I couldn't imagine going camping with a six-hundred-dollar phone, but I wanted to take pictures and video."

Ron came to stand behind Julie, one hand on her shoulder. "I like it, Reddy. I can't tell you how many times I've been out with a group, and somebody fumbles their damn phone. I tell them not to take pictures with their expensive tech, but somebody always does and regrets it."

"That's when we came up with the idea of tech rental as part of the package." Julie tapped Ron's hand excitedly, one red fingernail bobbing up and down. "They start off with you. They get the big stuff figured out, the boats and permits and tents and, you know. Stuff."

She waved a hand. "Then you send them to me. I help them with the things they forgot. A special shirt, an extra jacket or socks. Then I turn them over to my tech guy and get 'em set up with a phone and camera, returnable to us. We download the data to a memory stick and give it to them as a souvenir of their trip." She raised her hand.

Ron handed her a flash drive shaped like an oar. The blade end detached from the grip to reveal the tech. "Cool, hunh?" he said. "I found it on Amazon."

I'd heard the worried comments about expensive technology. We sold watertight containers and bags, but it was still a concern. What if you dropped the watertight container in a lake?

"You have a tech guy?" I asked.

Gideon raised his hand.

"You?"

"I was in the cyber-crime department. I know my way around a mobile phone."

"But you live in San Francisco."

He shrugged. "It's negotiable."

Julie stood, sliding her arm around Ron's waist. "Think about it, okay? I'll give you a call in a few days and we can talk in more detail. Maybe you'll want to run the idea past Reed and Rhea. They're a part of the future of your store." She nodded to Gideon. "Thanks." They moved away, pausing to stop at the bar.

"You set me up." I pointed an accusatory finger at Gideon.

He captured my hand. "She and I started talking when I went into her store, when I first got to town. I mentioned going on a canoe trip of some kind and she said that you were the one to talk to about that. We chatted then I mentioned I wanted a place to retire and how I wanted to figure out some kind of part-time job, something with computers. One thing led to another, and we had lunch. That's when she told me her ideas."

"Retire? Here? BFN?" I stared at him in astonishment.

"Maybe. And maybe a trip to Hawaii or Jamaica in January or February?" He eyed me hopefully.

Oh, man. Hawaii. Warm temps, green trees, and white sand beaches. "You shouldn't make any decisions until you experience a winter here," I warned.

He released my hand and picked up one of the brandy snifters, handing it to me. Then he took the other and raised it to me in a little salute.

"I'm sure you know a few ways to keep warm." He took a sip. "She's got a good idea."

"I'm not sure," I said. "Most of the people we get in the store are seasoned campers. I'm not sure how many would want that kind of thing."

"That's the point. You could expand your reach. I'm a city guy and it sounds great to me to have at least one night of a week of camping be handled for me."

"You're not exactly the typical city guy. You're an ex-parachute guy who's been a cop for thirty years and is in great shape."

"You think I'm in great shape?"

I flushed. "Well, yeah, maybe. You have to be in great shape to be a cop, right?"

"It depends on what you do. Desk jobs, no. Street work, yeah." He frowned. "Maybe that's why I hated the idea of desk work. I figured I'd get fat and happy."

"Somehow, I don't see you ever getting fat. Happy, maybe."

"I can live with that."

I sipped the brandy. It was warm in my throat, almost as warm as his smile. "I'll think about it," I conceded. "Her idea might have merit."

We sipped and sat for another hour, relaxing by the fireplace. Then we drove back to my house. Gideon parked the car in the drive and walked with me to the back door.

"I've been thinking about it," he commented. "Wasn't it confusing, the women in your family having the same name?"

I stopped, my hand on the doorknob. The sight of the door and the dark house made me remember the angry voice on the phone, the defaced front door.

I shook away the thought. "Oh, we didn't have the same name. Grandmother was always Red One. Mother was Red Two."

"And you're Reddy." He pulled me closer. I looked up into his eyes. "Right? You're Reddy?"

I hesitated. Was I ready?

I remembered Grandmother's pungent advice.

She was right.

"You bet I am."

Chapter 10

We made it to the couch in the living room, shedding clothing as we went. It had been several years since I was intimate with a man and at first I hesitated, wondering what he'd think when he saw my aging body.

Then I was lost in a wave of, well, lust. Gideon's hands awakened the slumbering passion I had banked for those years. When we fell onto the couch and his hand started to stroke me, I ignited. I'd forgotten how great it could feel to have a man who took his time and shared with me.

Forgotten? Who was I kidding? This might be the first time I had a man who appeared to relish me as much as I relished him. I resolved to enjoy every minute. We quickly dispensed with the issue of birth control (I had my tubes tied years ago) and safe sex (neither of us had a partner for several years) and we sank into pleasure.

At some point we moved upstairs, laughing as we went. Then I remembered the remains of my steak dinner and the takeout box I had left on the kitchen counter. I raced downstairs and stowed it in the fridge before the resident feline could sense it. I ran back upstairs and before hopping into bed, I cracked the window slightly.

"What are you doing?" Gideon demanded when I slid back under the covers.

"I like to sleep with fresh air."

"It's forty degrees out there! Are you crazy?"

I snuggled against him. "I can think of ways to stay warm."

"Oh, well, if you explain it that way…"

****

We slept late and when I woke, I dragged on a bathrobe and padded to the kitchen to call Reed.

"I'm taking a day off," I said while I fixed the coffee, mobile phone jammed between my shoulder and ear.

"Good for you. We're not supposed to get much but it'll be enough to make folks sit up and take notice."

I wasn't sure what he meant. Then I peeked out the window at the softly falling snow. "Yep, it'll remind people of what's coming."

"Have a good day. I'll handle things at the store."

"I know you will. Thanks, Reed." I hung up and turned. Gideon was coming into the kitchen dressed in his jeans and T-shirt. "I'm sorry. Did I wake you?"

He crossed the room, wincing at the cold floor on his bare feet. "Nope. You're taking a day off?"

I pointed to the window. "Snow day."

"Hmm." He stepped onto the kitchen rug and enfolded me in his arms. "What do you have in mind?"

"I'm sure I'll think of something."

We lounged around, watched the snow, made popcorn, made love, watched a movie, laughed. I couldn't remember the last time I had such a good time. It wasn't only the sex, which was great. I was relaxed, happy, and content. I'd have some pleasant memories to hold on to when Gideon left. It was fun.

It was after lunch that my doorbell rang. I was laughing at something Gideon said in response to a movie we were watching. I pulled open the door to find

Jake on the front step.

Before I could speak, he said, "I see you've had company for the night." His glare told me exactly what he meant.

"Are you keeping track of who I see and what I do?" I leaned against the doorframe, my arms crossed on my Mickey Mouse sweatshirt which matched my Minnie Mouse sweatpants. I was naked underneath my couture, but they were so baggy I doubted Jake could tell.

"If you'll recall, you filed a police report that someone was harassing you, so yes, we are keeping an eye on who's around."

My face got hot at this statement. I had completely forgotten about the doorknob rattling pest who'd bothered me the last few days.

"Thank you for the attention," I said with what dignity I could muster.

I thought he'd snap at me but instead he wheeled around and strode down my walk to the squad car in the drive. I sighed and closed the door.

"Problems?" Gideon asked when I sank back on the couch with him.

"No, I don't think so." I pushed the unpleasant encounter away by snuggling in with Hoody and Gideon under the afghan.

Grandmother called in mid-afternoon. "Do you folks want to meet us tonight for dinner and dancing? I know you've had a guest overnight, but do you think you can tear yourself away long enough to come out for Friday Funday?"

The Small-Town Gossip Line was obviously at work. I laughed at the sly humor in her voice.

"Let me check." I lowered the phone. "Do you want

to go out tonight with Grandmother and Woody for dinner and dancing?"

"Sure, I'm game if you are. I'm not much of a dancer, though."

"Neither am I. We can watch them and cheer them on." I raised the phone. "We're in. What time should we pick you up?"

"Five o'clock should be fine. We can have a cocktail before dinner. I'm looking forward to it, dear." She hung up.

I snuggled against Gideon. "Five o'clock. We'll pick them up at the CF and go out to the country club. It's a buffet every Friday night followed by dancing in the upstairs assembly room."

"I think I'll go back to the hotel and change. Then I'll return and pick you up." He kissed me quickly. "I may need a nap, too. You kept me busy last night."

"If you're available, I'll keep you busy tonight, too."

He grinned. "I'm available."

We untangled ourselves from blanket and paws and I walked him to the back door. He left, reluctantly, a few minutes later. I sailed upstairs and hopped in the shower. Gideon and I had showered earlier, but I wanted another long soak to luxuriate in the feeling of a body well used and loved. It had been years since I ached like this, and I enjoyed it.

I dried my hair then dressed in black jeans and a red and white sweater set, casual but dressy. My black low boots completed my couture. A dab of makeup and I was back downstairs in an hour, giving Hoody his evening meal and tidying up the house.

I stopped at the answering machine and stared at the message there. Delete it? No? Yes, I decided. I wanted no reminders of ugliness. I was having too much fun to have a black cloud hanging over my head.

A half hour later Gideon's rental car pulled into the driveway. I grabbed my cape and was out the door before he'd gone two steps. The inch or two of snow had mostly melted when the sun came out in the afternoon, so I minced around the slushy spots when I walked.

"Are we in a rush?" he asked, pulling me to him. He'd changed into jeans, a dark blue sweater and his tweed jacket.

"If I know Grandmother, they're waiting in the lobby, ready to go. They love their Friday Funday." I brushed a quick kiss against his lips then slipped my arms around his waist. I fit right under his chin.

"I suppose the sooner we go, the sooner we return," he murmured.

"You read my mind."

We drove to the CF and yes, the elderly dancers were waiting for us in the lobby. In the nearby dining room, I saw people shuffling in for their evening meal.

I walked between the two seniors, arms akimbo so they could grasp my elbows. I got them outside. Gideon left the parked car and helped Grandmother into the front seat while I got Woody settled in the back.

"Where to?" Gideon asked while we buckled up.

"The Perrault Country Club. Go to the street, take a right and I'll give you directions from there." Grandmother tucked her cane next to her and beamed at Gideon. "I'm so glad you youngsters decided to join us tonight. We always have such a marvelous time and tonight Reddy won't have to fend off her admirers, asking for a dance."

I laughed from the back seat where I sat behind

Gideon. "They're being polite. They don't like seeing me sitting there, admiring their dance moves." I turned to Woody. "I suspect you of bribing people to ask me to dance."

Woody put a hand on his chest. "I would never do that. I might suggest that some of the single gentlemen give you a turn around the dance floor, but I would never bribe anyone." He wore his usual Friday Funday attire of dress slacks, wingtip shoes, black V-neck sweater and a white shirt with a necktie.

Tonight's tie had dancing pumpkins on it. Woody had an amazing assortment of ties. 'A hobby of mine,' he confessed once. 'I love prowling through consignment stores. There are treasures to be found.'

"I enjoy watching you two out there on the dance floor," I said. "Those lessons you're taking are paying off."

"Rosie's a good partner. She lets me lead now and then." He winked at me.

"I can't hear what you're saying," Grandmother tossed over her shoulder.

"That's the point," I said. "We can have our secrets."

"Ooh, what are you plotting?" She tapped Gideon on the arm. "I'm worried, aren't you?"

"Not at all," he said easily. "They're no match for us."

She chuckled. "Good to know." She continued issuing directions as needed and soon we were at "the Club" where she and Woody each had a social membership, and I had a golf membership for the nine-hole course. The fees were low compared to courses in larger towns, so we had our share of visitors, especially during summer and the high tourist season that brought in people from the Twin Cities.

The course was beautiful in the setting sun with the gold and red trees on the hillsides, the fairways still green with snow nestled in shadows here and there. The clubhouse was older, a two-story rectangular building on the ninth green. The Friday buffet was served downstairs in the large bar area and dancing would take place upstairs in "the assembly hall", a big open space often used for weddings and class reunions.

We caused a bit of a stir when we walked in. Everyone knew Grandmother and Woody and me, but Gideon made several people turn their heads. The Mysterious Stranger.

We took a seat near the windows that overlooked the course and ordered drinks from the girl who came to the table. They had a good crowd. Forty or fifty people sat at the different tables and one long table was composed of ten couples who appeared in their mid-thirties.

Our drinks arrived and we relaxed, Grandmother whispering gossip to Gideon about the people around us. I watched him as she spoke. He was attentive, smiling at her innuendos and sometimes answering her with a comment that made her grin.

"He's a nice guy," Woody said, leaning close to me to be heard over the buzz of conversation around us.

"Yes, he is."

"Did you ask him about his job? About that stuff Jake told you happened?"

"I didn't have to ask. He volunteered the information." I quickly summarized what Gideon had told me about the shooting and subsequent fallout.

"I'm not surprised," Woody said. "I used to go to

conventions, and we'd get lots of folks from around the country. We usually had breakout groups for those of us in smaller towns, but sometimes we had a chance to chew the fat with guys from the bigger departments. That kind of crap goes on more than you'd think."

"What do you mean?"

He fiddled with the stir-stick in his drink, his blunt fingers swishing it this way and that. "Gideon was doing the right thing, and it might have made his boss look bad. There're all kinds of discrimination in big organizations, sometimes subtle, sometimes not so subtle. He stuck up for his partner, but it put him at odds with the higher ups. They wanted to sweep the harassment stuff under a rug."

Woody shot Gideon a sympathetic glance. "Change is hard sometimes. I was skeptical when we got a woman in the police department here in town. But she showed me she knew the job and I had to admit I was wrong. I had to keep an open mind and judge her against the same standards I'd use for a male officer. I had to change my way of thinking. It's hard to change an opinion you've held most of your life."

I considered what he said as we joined others in the line for the buffet, which was set up at the far side of the room. No matter how much people wanted to keep the status quo, life was a process of constant change. My mother had always counseled me to keep an open mind about any situation and she was absolutely right.

"You're thoughtful, dear," Grandmother murmured, holding her plate out so I could dish out a measure of green beans on it.

"I was thinking how odd life is sometimes. A week ago, we were visiting Mother's grave." I looked to my left, where Gideon and Woody were taking plates from the stack, Gideon eyeing the sliced ham in the serving tray. Woody said something and Gideon chuckled.

"A week ago, you didn't know he existed. And now you do." Grandmother shuffled forward, pausing by the next serving dish. I obediently ladled some mashed potatoes on her plate and drizzled them with gravy before serving myself.

"Life has a way of putting people and situations in our path. How we address them can be telling." She began to move away, her plate tilting precariously.

"Let me take that." I took her plate and mine and paced beside her while she made her way back to our table, pausing more than once to chat with someone. I made sure she was seated then set down our plates, going back to the buffet for butter and rolls.

"Isn't she dating Jake Grimly?" someone whispered behind me. It wasn't much of a whisper because I heard it plainly.

"I guess not," a male voice replied. "Of course, young folks today, they flit from one person to another, don't they?"

Young folks, I thought. Flitting. I resumed my seat and Gideon leaned over to ask, "What has you smiling?"

"I like being called a young person," I said.

"I get the feeling we're in the spotlight tonight." He cut into the slice of ham on his plate and took a bite. "Wow. That's good."

"Most of the food served here is local. That ham probably came from five miles away. Wait until hunting season gets underway and they have a venison cook-up. That's pretty good. And you can't miss the first big wall-eye fry-up in the summer. That's special."

"I'll mark my calendar." He stared into my eyes

when he said it and I had the feeling he'd do exactly that.

We lingered over our meal and coffee then went upstairs when we heard the music. Once a month a live combo took over the small stage, but tonight was one of the club employees, playing music on an ancient sound machine.

Woody led Grandmother out on the dance floor for a waltz then came for me when a rousing polka played. Gideon and Grandmother sat at the small table set off to one side, heads together and critiquing our style while we romped around the floor.

Two more hours of dancing and laughing ensued. At nine o'clock, Grandmother tapped my arm. "Time to take us home, dear. Much as I'd love to dance all night, these old bones aren't up to the excitement."

We bundled into coats then Gideon went out for the car, driving to the upper parking lot for Grandmother and Woody to enter. I sat in the front seat this time, turned to chat with them while he backed the car to drive along the winding road leading to the clubhouse.

The car's headlights swept over the expanse of golf course, trees casting long, dancing shadows when the wind moved them. Behind us at the clubhouse I saw someone silhouetted to the side of the doorway. I had the feeling they were watching us drive away.

Maybe somebody who slipped outside for a smoke, I decided, turning around. I checked the rear-view mirror and saw headlights come on in a car in the upper parking lot. Then we made a right turn out of the lane and the club was lost to sight.

I directed Gideon back to the CF and we escorted the dancers into the building. My grandmother enfolded me in a big hug. "Enjoy yourself, my dear. He's a marvelous young man." She kissed my cheek, her scent of powder and flowers surrounding me.

I hugged her in return. "I know. And I am enjoying myself, no matter how long it lasts."

She pulled away to regard me. "I have the feeling it will last as long as you want it to last. You have options." With a wave to Gideon, Grandmother looped her arm through Woody's, and they began a sedate walk into the facility.

Gideon and I drove to my house. I couldn't understand it, but I had an uncomfortable feeling, as though waiting for something to happen. He noticed because when we pulled into the drive, he said, "Can I come in? Or would you rather be alone tonight?"

I took his hand. "I don't know what's going on. I have the oddest feeling that something's not right. Of course I want you to join me tonight." I smiled but it was forced. I couldn't recapture the lighthearted casual happiness from an hour before.

We went into the house. I got out a bottle of wine, then Gideon and I joined Hoody on the sofa, cuddling together and watching TV. He didn't push me to speak, and I was grateful for his solid, comfortable presence. It could keep the boogie man at bay.

At ten o'clock the news came on and I turned off the set. "I never watch news," I said. "I hate going to bed depressed."

He nudged me. "Let's go make some sweet dreams."

We did just that and I fell asleep an hour later in his arms. I was deep into dreamland when my landline phone rang from the hallway at the top of the steps. I stumbled out of bed, leaving a warm cat and warm man behind me, shivering in the cool air.

"Reddy? This is Mrs. Velvet, out at Happy Home Care. Your grandmother is ill, and I wondered if you could come out."

I came awake with startling suddenness. "What? I saw her tonight. We went out dancing. She was fine."

"I know. She pressed her emergency call button a few minutes ago. She's very agitated and wants to see you. I notified the doctor who's on call and he's with her now."

"What is it?" Gideon stood in the doorway to the bedroom, a blanket around him.

"Grandmother. She's taken ill. I have to get to the CF." I was still holding the phone. "We'll get dressed and be there as soon as we can," I said, then I hung up. I whirled to go into the bedroom, panic making me stumble over my feet.

Gideon put his hands on my arms. "Take a deep breath. It'll be okay." He peered into my eyes, and I felt my anxiety start to ebb.

We dressed hurriedly and were out the door in fifteen minutes. Gideon drove through dark streets. It was almost one in the morning and the bars were still open, with a few cars parked in the lots we drove past. We didn't speak. I was too busy praying, and he was focused on unfamiliar roads.

He parked in the small visitor's lot at the CF, and we raced to the front door. One of the nursing aides was waiting for us and buzzed us in. "She's in her apartment," the girl said, gesturing us into the lobby.

I led the way along dimly lit hallways to the end then to the right. The facility was built like a big "C", with a courtyard in the middle. Grandmother's apartment was halfway to the end on the side facing into the courtyard, not out to the street. Her door was open, and I went in, Gideon right behind me.

Woody met me before I'd gone two steps. "It's okay," he said, stopping me in my tracks. "She had a bit of a scare. It must have been a nightmare because she said somebody was in here with her. She woke up and said that someone was near her bed."

"I thought she was sick." I moved past him in the small foyer area of her two-room unit. Straight ahead of us was the living room and immediately to the left was the 'kitchen', a sink, small fridge, and a few cupboards.

Grandmother's spacious bedroom was through a door on the right. I went to it and saw a man with her. I vaguely recognized him as one of the doctors from the community hospital. He stood near Grandmother's double bed, his hand on her arm where it lay outside the covers.

She wore her silky pajamas, the purple ones I bought her for Christmas. Her sheets were pale pink, and she appeared so faded against them.

The doctor turned when I entered the room. "See, she's here," he said, holding out an arm. "Everything's okay."

Grandmother struggled to sit up in bed and I hurried to her, sinking down to sit on the side of the bed. "It's okay," I said soothingly. "I'm here."

"Oh, thank God." She clutched my hand, grabbing it with surprising strength. "You're okay. She didn't get you."

"I'm fine, I'm fine." The doctor had moved away to make room for me. He stepped back to the bedroom's doorway where Woody and Gideon stood. "What happened? Mrs. Velvet said you were ill."

"No, it wasn't that. Well, yes, I was so surprised I thought I was having a heart attack or something. She was right there, standing right beside the bed. It scared me so much I couldn't even scream. How did she get in here?"

"Who? Who was here?"

"It was that girl, that Louise girl, the one from the courthouse." Grandmother still clung to my hands, hers trembling.

"Courthouse?" I looked back at Woody.

"Louise Wulfson," he said. "That's who she means."

"What? You saw her? Where?" I caught the disbelieving expression in Woody's eyes before I turned back to Grandmother.

"Right here." She released my hands and slapped the bed, narrowly missing my knee. "She was standing right here. That girl came into my room and was standing right there."

Nightmare, I thought. We've been talking about the accident so much lately. "Are you sure it was her? She's been gone a long time. She was a child back then."

"I know it was her. Right here. Right by my bed." Grandmother was starting to tremble again, bright patches of color on her pale cheeks.

"Calm down, Rosie," Woody said from behind me. "You're working yourself into another tizzy."

"You'd be in a tizzy too if you woke up and saw that awful girl glaring at you!" Grandmother struggled to sit up, but I gently pushed her back against her pillows.

"I'll check with the aide on duty. They must keep track of who comes in and who leaves." Gideon said something in a low voice to Woody then left the room. I glimpsed him in the living room, speaking with the doctor.

I knew they kept track of visitors. If Louise Wulfson was in the facility, someone would know. It had to be a nightmare. No way would anyone allow a stranger inside. The staff was careful because they didn't want an elderly person getting confused and wandering off. So the exterior doors had a keypad entry system with someone on duty at the front door to buzz in visitors.

"You don't believe me, do you?" Grandmother's voice was thin and reedy. For the first time in a long time, she seemed her age, frail and so old.

"I don't know," I said. "It's hard to believe. The staff here are so careful."

She touched my hand, giving it a quick squeeze. "I know what I saw."

I returned the squeeze. "I'll stay with you tonight. No one will bother you if I'm here." I shook my head when she started to protest. "I insist. I'm staying here." I gestured to the chaise in the corner of the room, her 'fainting couch' as we called it. "I've slept there before and it's comfortable." It wasn't but it was passable. "Give me a blanket and share one of your pillows and I'll be fine."

She relaxed immediately and I knew I said the right thing. "If you're sure…"

"Of course, I'm sure. I'll talk to the doctor now then I'll be right back." I stood, bending over to kiss her cheek. Woody moved in to take my place. I gave his shoulder a squeeze. "I'm staying here."

"Sounds good. I'll be here until you come back." He covered Grandmother's hand with his and she smiled tremulously at him.

I went into the living room where Gideon stood with the doctor and Mrs. Velvet, a buxom lady with steel gray hair and a no-nonsense demeanor.

"What happened?" I asked in a low voice.

"She pressed the panic button. I got here as fast as I could, within five minutes at the most." Mrs. Velvet lived in the facility with her husband, a large gentleman who did small maintenance chores for the fifty residents. Every unit had the so-called panic buttons installed in each room and each resident was required to wear one on a lanyard around their necks.

"The alarm sounds at the front desk and also in our apartment. I called the doctor as soon I heard it."

I turned to the doctor. "What's the verdict?"

"She had an erratic heart rhythm, not unusual when someone is frightened or panicked. She insists she saw someone next to her bed."

"There was no one here when I got here," Mrs. Velvet insisted. "There are no strangers wandering around this facility. We're careful about who we allow to come in and who we hire. It must have been a nightmare."

The doctor nodded agreement. "She said it was the anniversary of her daughter's death recently. Perhaps that caused it. As I understand it, this Louise person was involved, is that right? Or she was there when your mother died?"

"I don't think so," I said. "We were in an accident several years ago and I think my mother had complications from it and that caused her death. Maybe Grandmother is getting things confused."

Even as I said it, I had the strongest feeling I was

wrong. Why would she have nightmares now? Yes, it was the anniversary of the accident, but we'd had anniversaries before this with no ill effect.

"I want her to come to the clinic tomorrow and we'll run a few tests," the doctor said. "The staff here can bring her."

"Of course," Mrs. Velvet confirmed. It wasn't unusual for one of the staff to ferry a resident here or there. "What kind of tests?"

"I'll check her heart and maybe do a blood test. I'll review her records and see what might be needed."

"I think she'll rest easy now that you're here, dear," Mrs. Velvet said. "You'll stay here tonight?"

I turned to Gideon. He put an arm around me, and we moved away from the others. "I'm sorry, but I need to be with her," I murmured.

"Of course you do. Don't worry about it. I'll go back to my hotel. You call me in the morning, and I'll come get you." He gave me a quick kiss. "This is important. You need to stay with her and make sure she's okay."

The doctor and Mrs. Velvet joined us. "I'll walk out with you. Let me tell Woody." I ducked my head into the bedroom. "I'm going with Gideon to his car then I'll be right back."

Woody waved a hand. "We're doing fine. Take your time."

I said a mental thankful prayer that he was here and helping. If anyone could calm Grandmother, it would be Woody.

The doctor and Mrs. Velvet walked ahead of us through the silent hallway. "Give me a call when you're ready and I'll come to get you," Gideon said in a low, soft voice. "Do you need me to do anything at your house? Feed Hoody or anything like that?"

"He'll be fine, but thanks for offering." I looped my arm through his. "Thanks for everything. I'm sorry we had to cut our evening short."

"There'll be other evenings."

"Will there? Aren't you leaving soon?"

He glanced at me. "My plans are flexible. Woody said his buddies are reporting back tomorrow. Or today, I guess. It will depend on if they find anything."

I was surprised at my relief. I hadn't grasped how much his impending departure had preyed on my mind until I spoke the words. "Good. It's nice to have you here."

"It's nice to be here."

We got to the front door and the doctor left, nodding to me before exiting. Gideon kissed me quickly. "Call me when you're ready to go." He followed the doctor out the door and the two men headed for the parking lot.

Mrs. Velvet and I began our walk back through the hallways, pausing when we got to her apartment door. "Thank you for coming so quickly," she said softly. "Rosie was so anxious. I knew you'd help get her calmed right away."

"She's my only living relative. I want to keep her with us however long I can."

She patted my arm. "I know what you mean. Good night." She went into her apartment, the door closing softly behind her.

I went to Grandmother's apartment. Woody stood when I came into the room. "She's resting now."

I kissed his cheek. "Thank you."

He left. A light was still on in the living room. I found the spare pillow and blanket and made myself a little bed on the lounge, making sure my mobile phone was on mute. I closed the bedroom door slightly, leaving it ajar enough so the light illuminated Grandmother resting on the bed.

"Thank you, Rebeka," she whispered.

"I'm here if you need me."

"I know. Thank you."

I heard her deep sigh then the room sank into stillness. I found a comfortable position and dozed off.

I slept fitfully until six-thirty when my phone thumping my leg told me I had a call coming in. I was jerked completely out of sleep once again when the police officer on the line told me my store had been broken into.

Chapter 11

"I'm fine. You go and take care of things at the store. I'll see the doctor later today and I'll call you." Grandmother certainly appeared better. She had come out to the living room where I had gone to speak on the phone, pulling on her fluffy pink bathrobe.

"Are you sure?" I folded my blanket, tucking it and the pillow into the closet where I'd found them a few hours before.

"I am absolutely sure. A good night's sleep made all the difference." She made a shooing motion. "You go handle that."

I hesitated. I hated to leave her alone, but I was needed at the store. One of the officers cruising through downtown last night saw the front door of the store wide open. When he went inside to check, he said it looked like someone had upset the displays.

A real mess, he said.

"I can call Reed, and he can—"

"You go," Grandmother said firmly. "Do you need to call Gideon for a ride?"

I winced. "I hate to wake him up."

"I don't think he'll mind."

Well, I didn't have much choice. I kissed her then left her apartment, promising to be back in the afternoon in time to go with her to her doctor appointment. I hurried through the quiet hallway to the front door.

I decided not to call Gideon. The CF was only six blocks from the store. I could get there just as fast walking. I emerged into a cold morning and set off, my hands jammed into my jacket pockets. I was wearing sneakers, and they had good traction on the pavement slippery with frost from overnight.

I cut through the parking lot and moved along quiet streets, the town still sleepy on this Saturday morning. When I left the CF behind me a car pulled into the employee parking area, morning staff coming on duty.

The chilly air woke me up better than a cup of coffee. Dampness in the air made me wonder if snow was in the forecast. It was still early October, but we often had some dustings of snow during October. The Real Snow started falling in November and usually didn't let up until March.

Of course, with climate change everything was changing. I remembered Julie's idea of sharing our businesses. By the time I got to my store, I had decided it might be a good plan. But would Gideon be willing to stay around to be her tech guy?

I'd worry about that when the time came. Right now, I had a break-in to worry about. I came through the front door and the first person I saw was Jake, talking to a uniformed officer. They both turned when I entered, pausing to survey the damage.

The place was a real mess, but it wasn't as bad as I'd feared. The circular display racks holding sweatshirts had been thrown to the floor, the merchandise kicked around to the corners of the big main room.

The wooden checkout counter, inherited from the previous store when it was a dry-goods emporium, had been attacked. I couldn't think of any other word to describe it. The surface was dented and chipped, with gouges around the surface and in front. A discarded sledgehammer nearby told what had been used.

The old cash register which was only for show had been tossed on the floor and trampled. We used iPads for transactions and those were locked securely in my office. The ammunition and arrows were kept in locked cases with tempered glass, and they appeared to be unharmed. It was only the apparel that had taken damage.

I turned slowly. "Who did it?" I asked hoarsely.

Jake left the officer and came to stand with me. "We got some fingerprints on the sledgehammer and the front door."

I saw the blue powder on the doorframe. "Is this it? How about the back offices?" I tried to get past him, but he blocked my movement. "What?"

"The back rooms weren't touched. What's going on, Reddy? Why is someone doing this to you?" His brown eyes were accusing and that more than anything pissed me off.

"How should I know? Isn't that your job? To figure out who's got it in for me?" I glared at him, clenching and unclenching my fists.

His gaze raked me up and down. I know what I looked like. I'd thrown on the first thing that came to hand a few hours earlier when I got the call about Grandmother. Wrinkled sweatshirt, wrinkled jeans, and sneakers. It was obvious I slept in my clothes.

"Your new friend appears to be keeping you busy," he said frostily.

As if on cue, my phone rang from my back pocket. I pulled it out and saw Gideon's name on the display. Jake saw it, too, because he muttered something and shot me an icy glare.

I stepped away from him and went to a corner of the store, putting the phone to my face. "Hey, did you get any sleep?"

"A little. Do you need me to come pick you up?"

"I'm at the store. Somebody broke in last night. The cops called me an hour or so ago. I walked over here. It's not that far from the CF." I sighed. "I need to call Reed and Barb to come help me clean up."

"Is it bad? What was taken?"

"I don't think anything was taken. Somebody came in and kind of trashed the place. Hold on." I lowered the phone. "Can I have my staff come in and help me clean up? Do I need to close for the day?"

"We'll be done in a few minutes," the officer said. "You'll need a new lock for the front door. The old one was busted out."

"Okay." I raised the phone again. "I'll be busy this morning going through everything. I'll give you a call later and let you know how it's going."

"Let me know if I can help with anything. I talked to Woody, and he said to come by after lunch. He and his friends are doing a Zoom call this morning and he said they had some solid leads."

He sounded hopeful but I barely noticed. My mind was racing, trying to decide what to worry about first. "I need to go with Grandmother to the doctor this afternoon. We can go out to the CF together if you'd like."

"Sure. I'll pick you up around twelve-thirty. Call me later if that doesn't work."

"Okay. Thanks." I ended that call and dialed Reed's number. I told him what had happened, and he promised to be there in a few minutes. I didn't have Barb's phone number stored, but I decided that Reed and I could handle the mess until she arrived, so it didn't matter.

The police officer was at the front door, waiting for me. Jake had apparently left while I was on the phone and I was glad of it. Otherwise, he and I would have had an all-out argument.

The officer gave me some wipes that I could use to remove the fingerprint powder then he handed me his card.

"We'll call once we have any results from the prints," he said. "It seems like it was vandalism. You let us know if you find that something was stolen."

I said I would then he left. I began picking up discarded clothing and was hard at it when Reed arrived. I called the locksmith we used, and he promised to be there by early afternoon. Reed and I tidied up as best we could and by ten o'clock, we were almost back to normal.

I taped a hand-printed, "Opening Late" sign on the door after Reed and I surveyed our progress.

"Who would do this?" He began sorting shoes that had been flung around the small shoe area, which now looked like an angry toddler had gone on a rampage.

"I don't know. I've been in business for years and we've never had a lick of trouble. I don't get it."

Barb came in the back door. "Somebody at the gas station said there were police cars here. What happened?" She hung up her jacket in the back room and joined me.

"Somebody apparently didn't like my taste in apparel because he or she broke in and showed us what they thought." I picked up the pile of T-shirts that had been flung out of the cubbies on the wall, taking the pile to the counter to fold them. "I was with Grandmother last night when I got the call."

"Your grandmother?" Reed straightened, two hiking boots in hand. "Is everything okay?"

"I hope so. She had a bad nightmare last night and it shook her. They called me and I went over there to stay with her."

"How did the staff know to call you?" Barb asked, taking a T-shirt from the stack.

"Hmm?"

"Well, it was only a bad dream. How did the staff know she had a problem?"

"Oh, the panic button." I touched my throat. "All the residents wear them. It sounds an alarm. There's a couple who are full-time caretakers there and Mrs. Velvet came right away."

"Your family sure is lucky."

"You think so?" I folded another shirt. "It feels like I've had nothing but bad luck lately." Then I remembered Gideon. "Well, not all the time."

Barb had her back to me as she folded another shirt. "You walked away from that bad accident. I heard about it. You were sure lucky."

"We didn't exactly walk," I snapped. "We were hurt. Each of us."

"Sure, but you survived. Not everybody walks away from things."

I was too tired to argue with her. "Sure. Lucky." Reed was frowning at Barb. I thought of Rhea, who had survived her accident but would limp for the rest of her life. "I guess we need to count our blessings."

He switched his attention to me. "You bet."

We were able to open the store at eleven. We were local celebrities, and several townspeople came by to commiserate with me. Even Julie stopped and offered a replacement clothing rack for the one that had been mangled. We chatted briefly about her idea and decided to have lunch the next week to talk about it in more detail.

Gideon appeared at noon, coming through the front door and pausing. "You can hardly tell there was a problem," he said. "You guys work fast."

"It wasn't bad," I said. "Somebody maybe got drunk and decided to have some fun."

"Weird idea of fun," Reed muttered.

"There are weird people in the world." I pulled on my jacket. "I'm going out to the CF to go with my grandmother to her doctor appointment. Can you and Barb handle things while I'm gone?" I turned around. "Where is she?"

"I sent her out to get some more duct tape and some PVC piping so I could fix that one rack. She was doing that then she's getting lunch. She'll cover for me while I run out and get a sandwich to eat at the counter."

"She can cover for you to go home if you want to," I said, zipping up. "You don't have to eat here."

He hesitated, eyes going to Gideon. I moved to one side and Reed went with me. "I'm not sure I'm comfortable letting her manage the store without somebody here."

Oh, Lord. Now what? Didn't I have enough on my plate? I considered and discarded some replies then said, "You know better than me, Reed. You've worked with her this week. Do what you think is best."

He was so relieved I knew I'd chosen the right

words. "Okay, good. You go take care of your grandmother. I'll handle things here."

"I know you will. Thanks."

I left with Gideon, blinking in the sunlight. I had been so busy with the store I didn't even register that the sun had come up, much less how bright and warm it was compared to my early morning walk. I paused before getting into the car, drinking in the sight of the brilliant trees lining the street.

"It's so pretty at this time of year," I said, buckling up. "I know people who come up here to peep at the leaves and stay because they fall in love with this." I waved at a beautiful maple, bright red and swaying in the breeze.

Gideon backed out of the parking space. "It's easy to fall in love with," he said softly. "It's beautiful." He had a speculative expression in his pale blue eyes.

I was unaccountably flustered. In the back of my mind, I'd labeled him as *temporary*. But what if what we had wasn't temporary? Was I ready to have a man in my life? I had said good-bye to Doug with few regrets. Did I want to welcome someone to share with me now?

"You should have called," he chided softly. "I would have come to get you."

"It's a few blocks." I pointed ahead. "See, it's right there. I needed to wake up and an early morning walk was just the thing." I ran a hand over my jeans. "I wouldn't mind changing my clothes, though. I slept in these duds and I'm feeling grimy."

"We'll go back to your place once we talk with Woody and check on your grandmother. You must be beat. Did the police have any idea who broke into your store or why?" Gideon drove into the parking lot at the

CF, parking in almost the same spot as the night before.

"There were fingerprints. The asshole who did it used a sledgehammer on our old wooden counter and left the sledgehammer behind."

Gideon winced. "No wonder it appeared so beat up."

"I don't get it. Why is somebody causing me grief?" I got out of the car, waiting for him to join me to walk to the front door. "It's not like I have enemies. At least, not that I know of. Somebody rattles the doorknob at my house, they call and leave nasty voice mail, break into the store. What the hell is going on?"

Gideon didn't answer, but I didn't expect him to. I was only griping. We entered via the front door of the CF where a receptionist waved us in. Most of the tables were empty in the lunchroom, two or three people lingering over their meals. I wasn't surprised. Grandmother had complained about how early meals were served, with lunch beginning at eleven-thirty and dinner at five.

"Where are you meeting Woody?" I asked Gideon.

"His apartment. Can you show me the way?"

"Sure, it's near Grandmother's apartment. I'll dip in and check on her then join you." We hurried through the hall, and I stopped in front of Woody's door, the one decorated with a bright orange pumpkin drawing that had been colored by his grandchildren.

Woody opened it as soon as I knocked. His apartment was similar to my grandmother's apartment except his kitchenette was on the right and his bedroom was on the left. Woody's home was very masculine with dark furniture and wooden end tables, compared to my grandmother's pastel overstuffed sofa and her fragile-appearing maple side tables.

"Come on in." Woody stepped to one side, and we entered his little foyer.

"I need to check on Grandmother," I said. "I'll be right back."

"She went to the doctor," Woody said. "I knocked on her door before lunch, but I saw a note there saying she went to the clinic." He shut the door behind us and shooed us ahead of him into the living room.

"She was going this afternoon."

"Maybe they had a cancellation, and she got in early." He went into the apartment. We followed, taking spots on the couch. Woody took a seat opposite us and picked up his laptop from the coffee table.

"I wrapped up my call with the boys," he said, tapping a few keys. "Let me first explain how we found what we found. Gideon, it seemed like your stepdaughter's death might have had to do with her transplant, so we examined the hospital and the doctors." He regarded us over the laptop screen, his hazel eyes intent.

"I did, too." Gideon had changed into a blue plaid flannel shirt and jeans. The colors brought out the colors of his eyes and emphasized the salt-and-pepper of his hair. A line of sunlight filtered through the curtains, highlighting his face. "I tried that, too, but I didn't see any anomalies. It was hard to tell, though. There are so many transplants done and so many variables."

Woody busied himself with the laptop, poking at keys. "Yeah, we know. We took a different tack. You said she died of a heart attack, and she was relatively young. We narrowed it to only Minnesota at first. Some of the guys studied heart attacks in anyone who had a transplant." He peered at us over the gray lid of the laptop. "Then we tried to narrow it to young people. That didn't pan out."

"What did pan out?" I asked.

Woody set the laptop aside and leaned forward, hands clasped. They trembled slightly. "You knew this, didn't you, Gideon?" he asked, his voice also trembling.

Gideon straightened. "What do you mean?"

"You knew this. That's why you came here."

My gaze bounced from Woody to Gideon, confused. "What are you saying?"

"You knew about the transplant deaths." Woody kept his eyes fixed on Gideon.

"I'm not sure what you mean," Gideon said cautiously.

"He's a liar," Woody said emphatically. "He's lying."

I saw him tremble again. What I had viewed as old-age palsy was actually rage. This was the cop, the grizzled veteran who was interrogating someone, trying to get at the truth.

"What are you saying?" I had a horrible, sinking feeling in my stomach.

Gideon stood abruptly, walking to the window and staring at the enclosed courtyard. His hands were jammed into his pockets and his shoulders hunched. I recognized that posture. I'd seen him do it before, when he was trying to avoid thinking about something. Then he turned and faced us.

"You're right. I found the pattern," he said. "I knew something was off about Mindy's death. She was an athlete, in the prime of life. There's no way she would have a heart attack. I did the things your team was doing. I checked the doctor involved, the hospital, the donor.

That's when I found it."

"What?" I demanded.

"All recipients of Mrs. Wulfson's organs have died." Woody had his eyes fixed on Gideon, his face a harsh mask of anger. "And they each died on October 7." He jabbed a finger at the floor. "Today. The anniversary of her death." His voice was accusatory and once again I heard the cop interrogating a suspect.

"Holy shit," I whispered.

"I think someone killed your mother." Gideon nodded when I stared at him in astonishment. "She died on October 7. Of a heart attack. When she was alone. The same as the other donor recipients."

"How did you—what did—when did you—" I wasn't sure what I was asking.

Gideon came back to sit next to me, his attention going from me to Woody. "I'd been doing the research using my personal time but using department resources. I went to my captain with what I found. He—we didn't see eye to eye. It was what he needed to get me reprimanded and put on probation. I wasn't supposed to use police resources for a personal vendetta."

Gideon's lips twisted in a parody of a smile. "That's what he called it. Nothing I said convinced him. He wouldn't act on anything I found." His gaze went to Woody. "Office politics." Some message passed between the two men.

"Yeah, I've seen that," Woody said gruffly. "So you went to the Feds and that's when the shit hit the fan."

"The Feds?" I didn't believe what I was hearing. "The FBI? How did you know about it?" I asked Woody.

"One of the guys on the team. He's a retired Feeb. He put out some feelers. That's when we discovered you were playing us."

"I wasn't playing you," Gideon said. "I did need help." He shifted and I had the feeling he was trying to weigh what to say. "One of the organ recipients had the surgery in Wisconsin, so technically the crime crossed state lines. But I was in California and Mindy died in Missouri and I had no jurisdiction anywhere."

He shrugged. "I had to do some talking to get anyone to listen to me. In the end, I was suspended in California for stepping out of line. A junior agent in St. Paul agreed there were coincidences surrounding Wulfson's wife, but not enough for an official investigation."

"That's why you came here, hoping to gather the evidence they would need to get involved." Woody sat back in his chair, and I wondered how long he'd known about this. What else wasn't being said here? I had the sense that there were nuances at play, some kind of secret understanding between the two men that I wasn't privy to.

A knock sounded on the apartment door. Woody started to his feet, but I held up a hand. "I'll get it." I strode through the foyer and opened the door.

Mrs. Velvet stepped inside. "Oh, good, I wanted to talk with you," she said, seeing me. "Trudy at the front desk said you were here. Did you take your grandmother to the clinic? You need to check out when you do that. You shouldn't just leave a note on her door."

"What? No, I didn't. I came here to go with her. You said one of the people from here was going with her and I thought I'd go with them." I turned to Woody. "You said something about a note on her door?"

Mrs. Velvet clasped her hands nervously. "Yes, I

sent one of our aides to her apartment, but she isn't there. I know she was there earlier because the florist delivered some flowers to her apartment. The girl came in with the delivery and Trudy escorted her to your grandmother's apartment. They were beautiful flowers. I assumed you sent them."

I pushed past her to the hallway, striding to Grandmother's door. A note was taped to the door, written in block print: *Gone to the clinic, returning soon.* I knocked but no answer. I tried the knob, but it was locked.

Mrs. Velvet hurried after me, pulling a key ring from a pocket. Without a word she opened the door. A large bouquet of flowers lay on the small kitchen counter, the blooms hanging into the sink like the bouquet had been tossed there, haphazardly.

"Grandmother?" I called. "Did you get back from the doctor?" I went into the living room and from there to the bedroom. The bed was made. Grandmother always made her bed first thing in the morning as soon as she rose and today was apparently no exception despite the fuss of the night before.

"Pretty flowers," Gideon said behind me. "When did you have time to send them? You've been busy with the break-in all morning."

"What break-in?" It was Woody's voice.

I came out of the bedroom. Mrs. Velvet, Woody, and Gideon were in the living room. "My store was broken into last night," I said. "I didn't send the flowers."

Gideon went to the bouquet and picked it up. "No card." He and Woody once again exchanged that glance that told me something was up, that they had some kind of secret. I started to ask about it then Mrs. Velvet said,

"Let me call the clinic and see if she's there. Perhaps there's been a mix-up of some kind."

"What do you mean? If I didn't take her and no one from here took her, how would she get to the clinic?" But she had already turned away, reaching for her mobile phone and my question went unanswered.

"I don't understand any of this," I muttered. "My shop broken into, a threatening phone call, that thing with Grandmother last night. I feel like my life has gone off the rails." I turned on Gideon. "What aren't you telling me? You're holding something back."

"Like Woody said, there were pieces to the puzzle." His voice was low, so soft I had to lean near him to hear. "There were victims throughout the Midwest. Only one person survived the attacks. She had a cornea transplant but was still recovering."

"An eyewitness? Someone could identify the killer?" The idea was still stunning.

"Her vision was blurry, and she couldn't describe who did it clearly."

Mrs. Velvet rejoined us, pocketing her phone. "Your grandmother hasn't been there. The clinic called an hour ago to make an appointment, but no one answered. I think I need to contact the police." Her plain, angular face reflected distress and worry about the CF, which was responsible for the patrons there.

"I was going to call them," Woody said gruffly. "I think I know what happened. Can you let me handle it?"

"I'm not sure. Our residents are my concern." Mrs. Velvet lifted her phone again. "I don't know if I should do that."

I touched her arm. "We'll handle it. The police will include you in on anything we discuss. Please. It's possible this is a misunderstanding. I'd rather not upset the other residents if we don't need to."

That argument did the trick. Mrs. Velvet turned to Woody. "Are you certain?"

"As sure as I can be. You let me handle this for now. I know Rosie better than anybody. I'll find her. We'll talk to the police and have them come out here, quiet-like, so we don't get folks in an uproar." Woody walked her to the door, and she left, then he came back to us.

"It's time for you to tell the truth." His voice was harsh and angry when he confronted Gideon, a complete change of personality from the gentle, caring, solicitous old gentleman he'd been a moment before. "Someone took Rosie. That's right, isn't it?"

"What? Who took her?" I longed to shake someone.

"Let's go." Woody led the way out of Grandmother's apartment, back to his own. I spied Mrs. Velvet at the end of the hallway at the intersection in deep conversation with one of the aides. Then we entered Woody's apartment, and he turned to face us. "Tell us the truth."

Gideon shook his head. "I'm not sure. I know someone has it in for the people who received Mrs. Wulfson's organs and tissue. But I don't know why they came after Mrs. Davis."

Mrs. Davis. Grandmother. I began to understand. "You think someone took my grandmother? Why? I don't understand."

Woody paced his small living room, face bunched in thought. Then he stopped and turned. "The deposition," Woody said. "Damn it, that's it."

"What deposition?" "What deposition?" Gideon and I spoke at the same moment.

"Reddy, you were in the hospital. You and your mother were both too banged up to know about it. Wulfson raised a stink about his wife being an organ donor. The clerk at the driver's license bureau swore that Mrs. Wulfson signed the donor forms. The clerk said Mrs. Wulfson signed them after talking with your grandmother, who was there at the same time."

"What? Grandmother never mentioned that to me. Are you sure?"

"I remember it," Woody said. "Rosie was at the hospital and heard the fuss Wulfson was kicking up. She told him and the nurse with him about it, how she was getting her license renewed a year or two earlier. Mrs. Wulfson was there, and she was confused about the donor forms. Rosie talked to her about it and Mrs. Wulfson signed them. That's how they knew to get the clerk from the license bureau. Rosie had to go before a judge and swear to what Mrs. Wulfson did."

"She never told me that," I muttered, my mind whirling with the implications. I turned on Gideon. "Damn it, Jake was right. He told me to be careful about you."

"Hell, you were in and out of consciousness," Woody said. "By the time you got out of the hospital, it was over. It was only one more thing that happened back then. Gideon knew you were the only ones left, you and your mother and your grandmother. Isn't that right?"

Gideon seemed stunned and I realized he had miscalculated. "You thought he'd come after me, didn't you?" I demanded. "Is that why you stuck so close to me since you got here?"

The chagrin, the embarrassment in Gideon's eyes was enough answer for me. I took two steps forward and slapped him so hard his head snapped back.

"If anything happens to my grandmother, I'll kick your ass into Canada," I snarled through clenched teeth. "This was never about your stepdaughter, was it? This was some kind of pissing contest you had with your ex-boss."

He grabbed my wrist, jerking me around to face him. "This is about Mindy. And now it's about you and your grandmother. Everything changed once I met you."

"Yeah, right." I yanked my arm away from him and whirled, squeezing my eyes shut against the pain.

"I'm sorry," he said behind me.

I sucked in a harsh breath. "Yeah. I am, too."

"I'm sorry I hurt you. I'm not sorry about us."

I turned. "There is no us."

Chapter 12

"Reddy—"

I waved my hand. "Forget it. We have other more important things to worry about."

I turned to Woody. "What do we do now?" I groped for a chair, my knees wobbly. I was in shock.

I think. Or maybe I was so mad I couldn't see straight. What a sap I'd been. How stupid of me. I should have listened to my instincts when I said he was temporary. All of this bullshit with Gideon was just that.

Bullshit.

I shook that out of my mind, pushing away the lies, the pretenses. Grandmother was what mattered.

"It can't be Wulfson," I muttered. "Let's go to the police station. Woody, I'll drive your car. Gideon, you meet us there."

"I can drive," he said quickly. "My car's outside."

"No." I jumped to my feet. "I'll drive Woody and me. We'll meet you there." I didn't dare look at him. If I did, I might slap him again. I held out my hand and Woody fished the keys out of his pocket, dropping them in my palm. "Let's go."

I stalked to the door and the two men followed me. Instead of going through the facility, I made a left to go out the side door where the residents parked their cars. I heard Woody talking in a low voice to Gideon then the old man hurried after me. I peeked over my shoulder and saw Gideon jogging down the corridor in the opposite direction, heading for the front parking lot.

"What the fuck is going on?" I grumbled, pausing at the exit to tap in the security code at the alarmed door. Grandmother and I often used this door because it was closer to her apartment than going out the front. The staff kept me posted about the code whenever it changed.

"Somebody has it in for your family," Woody said, limping next to me. "I can't figure out who, though. Wulfson has been in prison and there's nobody else."

I slowed even though I longed to run to his big old Buick and throw myself into the driver's seat. "He had a kid," I said.

"She was adopted a few years ago and moved out of state. Wulfson didn't have any close friends, so it can't be that. Somebody has a vendetta because of Mrs. Wulfson, but I can't figure out who."

We got to the car, and I slid into the driver's seat, quickly adjusting it for my shorter frame. "How long have you known?" I asked, backing out and driving around the facility to the front. "How long have you known that he was lying?"

"I wondered." The old man glared straight ahead, his cheeks pink with anger. "Nobody shows up here because of such a tenuous connection. He did his research before he came here. I figured he wanted to talk to Wulfson, get the lay of the land, see if one of Wulfson's friends could be the one. The murderer."

Murderer. There it was. Blunt and true. Somebody was murdering people because they were fortunate enough to receive an organ donation.

"How many people has he killed? Three? Four?" I wasn't sure how organ donations were handled.

"Seven."

I almost slammed on the brakes. "What? Seven people?" We had reached the front, and I drove past Gideon, who fell in behind us. I didn't glance at him when we passed.

"Heart. Lung. Liver. Kidney. Pancreas. Tissue. Eyes." He ticked the words off on his fingers. I shuddered then remembered the John Prine song, "Please Don't Bury Me." His flippant recitation of body parts to cut up and share echoed in my head.

"Those are the ones my team found. There might be more. Tissue donation isn't as straightforward as the others. Some of that can be banked for future use, like for fire victims, or to repair hearts and stuff." Woody grunted. "I've learned more about how the human body works in the last few days than I really wanted to know."

"Why? Mrs. Wulfson signed the donor forms. Why retaliate against the recipients? And who's doing it? When did it start?"

"Two years after the accident. The first victim was the heart transplant person, a man in Rochester. They did the transplant at Mayo Clinic. He got the heart right after the accident and died two years later. Like Gideon's stepdaughter."

Woody was staring at me, but I kept my gaze straight ahead. "We're not sure about the tissue recipients," he said. "That can go throughout the U.S. because they can store it for later use. The organs, though, mostly went to people in Minnesota because it's near where she died."

The police station was straight ahead. I pulled the car into a parking space and turned it off. "This is crazy. Will Jake even believe this? The Feds didn't believe it.

Why would he?"

"The Feds might take it a bit more seriously now that my team is involved." Woody smiled when he saw my surprised expression. "Yeah, well, when a retired Feeb says there's a problem, people tend to sit up and notice."

"I hope Jake does." I opened the car door and waited for Woody near the curb. Gideon pulled in a few spaces away. I took Woody's arm, and we went to the main door, Gideon hurrying behind us.

Jake stood near the front desk. "I was getting ready to call you." His gaze went past me to Gideon and whatever he saw made him stare. "We ran the prints, and we know who broke into your store."

"My grandmother is missing," I said, overriding whatever else he wanted to say.

"What? When? We didn't get a report." He turned to check with the person behind the desk. The man shook his head.

I explained quickly about the nightmare the night before and her supposed doctor appointment this morning. Woody and Gideon flanked me, watching Jake absorb what I said.

"She's missing and no one knows where she is," I finished. "She doesn't drive anymore so someone must have taken her."

"I think it was Boyd Wulfson," Gideon said. "Woody and I have been following up on some leads about old murders."

"Murders that appeared like natural cause at first," Woody offered. "But once you start digging, it's mighty suspicious."

"It can't be Wulfson," Jake said. "We had him in the

211

drunk tank."

"What?" My heart sank. In the back of mind, I had hoped it would be straightforward. Wulfson had a peeve so he was taking it out on me and Grandmother.

"Like I said, we ran those prints and they're Wulfson's. He didn't even try to hide it. In fact, he told me he got drunk, trashed your place, then came here to confess."

"Here?"

"I had him in a cell until an hour or two ago. Him and Ozzy were there most of the night."

I sighed. "Ozzy?"

"Yeah. He was singing up a storm on Main Street. His daughter came and got him out in late morning."

"What about Wulfson's daughter?" Gideon asked. "She's in town, right?"

Jake shrugged. "She didn't come for him. His truck was parked over at the grocery store. He told me he'd walk over there and go home." He turned slightly, giving Gideon a cold shoulder. "Come to the back with me. We'll fill out a report for your grandmother."

"Report?" I almost slapped him, too. "We need to find her, not process paperwork."

"We normally don't start a search this fast, but for an elderly person—" His voice faded away in front of me.

"She didn't just wander off. Somebody took her."

Woody put an arm around my shoulders and gave me a little shake. "It'll only take a minute. Let's go."

I followed Jake, grumbling, Woody by my side. We got to Jake's office, Gideon following us. I turned to glare at him. "What do you think you're doing?"

"You might need me to explain what's going on."

His voice was calm, but his blue eyes were anything but that. They were cold and confident. The cop, I thought. This was his Cop Expression. I shivered.

I grabbed one of the two guest chairs. Woody took the other one. Gideon stood behind and between us, staring at Jake, who pulled over a keyboard and tapped a few keys.

"Tell me what happened," he said.

I started to speak but Woody overrode me. I began to object then I noticed that Woody was reciting the facts in a particular order as Jake typed, filling in some kind of online form. I subsided, conscious of Gideon at my back. I knew if I turned my head I'd be face-to-belt with him.

Was it only a few hours ago that I thought he was a Good Guy and might be a permanent fixture in my life? I was such a sap. Woody was right. Why would anybody come to Bum Fuck Nowhere on the off chance he could talk to someone and find out how his stepdaughter died?

Why didn't I see that? Why did I trust him? Why did I believe him?

Was any of it true? Was he truly an ex-cop? Then I remembered Jake had done a background check. Okay, that part was true, but what about the rest of it, his squabble with his superiors, the harassment thing, his partner?

I hunched my shoulders then deliberately relaxed. None of that mattered. All that mattered was finding Grandmother.

Woody finished his recitation. Jake typed a few more words then turned to us. "What's your story?" He directed the words to the man behind me.

"My stepdaughter died two years ago in what I

considered to be a suspicious manner. I investigated and found that others had died in a similar fashion. They died on October 7. Long story short, what I found led me to Perrault and Boyd Wulfson." Gideon spoke in a clipped manner, his words snapped out like little bullets.

"Part of his 'long story short' is that I'm on a team of retired law enforcement people and we examine cold cases." Woody spoke quickly. I think he was worried that Jake might discount anything Gideon said on general principle. "We investigated what he said, and we found it made sense. Boyd Wulfson's wife was an organ donor. The people who received her donated organs have died. On October 7."

Jake leaned back in his chair, his gaze shifting from Woody to Gideon. "Why didn't you go to the authorities with this?"

"I tried," Gideon shot back. "I didn't have the full picture, the one that Woody and his friends got. I had a couple of coincidences. No one listened to me."

Jake was silent, his eyes fixed on Gideon. I guess he believed what he saw because he stood. "I'll go talk to Boyd Wulfson and see if he can tell me anything about this."

"Talk? Are you crazy?" I leaned forward. "My grandmother is missing."

"I'll have one of our officers go to the nursing home and talk to the people there and talk to the people at the clinic."

I jumped to my feet. "The people at the clinic have nothing to do with this. Someone took my grandmother, Jake, and it wasn't Boyd Wulfson. I can help. Maybe he wants me."

He stepped forward and I forced myself to stay still

and meet him, chin to chin. Well, my chin to his chest.

"This isn't a game," he said. "This isn't a TV show. If you get put in harm's way, you'll be hurt, Reddy. And I'm not going to responsible for causing that."

Jake glared past me, his face set and hard. "That goes for you, too. You might have been some hotshot cop in California but you're a civilian here. You don't belong here."

Unspoken but said was *You don't belong here with Reddy.* I tried again. "Jake, please. It's my grandmother. I can't lose her, too."

His gaze shifted from Gideon to me. "This is my job, Reddy. Let me do it. I'll keep you posted on what we find." He gestured and I reluctantly led the way out of the room.

Jake stopped at the front desk, but I stomped past. I sensed Woody and Gideon behind me. I was so upset I barely noticed them. Facts, speculation, fear, and panic swirled in my head. I didn't see where I was going until I almost tripped on the front step.

Gideon grabbed my arm, keeping me upright. I jerked my arm away, not sure who angered me more, Gideon or Jake.

"What does he think he's doing?" I fumed.

"His job." Gideon's clipped tone told me how much he hated saying it.

"But—"

"Come on. Let's go. We need to figure this out. We'll meet at your house." I began to protest but he held up a hand. "We need to re-group and go over the data we have."

"He's right," Woody said. "The best thing we can do for Rosie is to think this through. Let Jake talk to

Wulfson. He'll call us if he finds out anything useful." Woody nodded decisively. "Let's go."

I hesitated. "Okay. My house." I hurried down the steps but stopped when I saw Gideon was helping Woody. "Sorry."

Woody waved me away. "That's okay. Get the car started."

I raced to the car and had it going by the time Woody slid into the passenger seat. "I'm not as fast as I used to be," he wheezed, buckling his seat belt.

"I'm sorry. I'm just anxious."

"I know you are." He put his hand on mine where it rested on the gear lever between us. "We'll find her, Reddy. I know we will."

I couldn't answer. I had too much emotion rattling around to form a coherent sentence. We drove in silence to my house, and I parked in the drive. Gideon parked on the street and came to meet us at the back door.

Hoody was waiting for us. I pushed past him and went to the living room then wheeled around and went to the phone charger on the kitchen counter. I plugged in my mobile and almost tripped over the cat.

"Dammit, cat, give me a break." He skittered away, hissing.

Gideon came in behind me. "I'll feed him."

I started to protest then shook my head. "Whatever." I stalked into the living room, my fists clenched. I heard a cupboard door opening and the sound of kibble going into a dish.

Woody followed me. "Why don't you change clothes and wash your face while I make us some coffee. I think we could each use a cup."

"I can do it. I need something to eat, too. I missed

breakfast." I started for the kitchen, but Woody put a hand on my arm.

"We'll handle it. You go and freshen up." He smiled encouragingly.

He was right. I wasn't sure what we'd be involved in, but I was pretty sure a flimsy sweatshirt and sneakers weren't the best thing to wear when facing a possible visit to Boyd Wulfson. The one time I'd seen it from a distance his ramshackle house was at the end of a rutted, twisting lane.

Boots, I decided. Hiking boots. I dashed upstairs. Ten minutes later I was back downstairs, now wearing a flannel shirt under a heavy dark green sweater and my heavier-weight jeans with my hiking socks.

The two men were in the kitchen. Hoody was at his food bowls, munching and purring. Woody nudged a plate to me.

"Thanks." I bit into a bologna sandwich and my stomach rumbled with pleasure. "I needed this," I said, picking up a potato chip from the bag on the counter. "Aren't you eating?"

"I had lunch at the CF." He went into the dining room, and I followed, Gideon behind me, a plate in his hand.

Woody pulled out a chair. "Here's what we know. Rosie was there this morning at ten o'clock because I talked to her. I went to her apartment, and she was in the living room, having a cup of tea."

"Mrs. Velvet said the flowers arrived at eleven o'clock." Gideon picked up the narrative. "The delivery girl was escorted by the receptionist to your grandmother's door then she had to leave and get back to the front desk. The delivery girl could find her own way out."

Gideon finished his sandwich and pushed his plate away. "The clinic called around eleven to make an appointment, but no one answered their call. We were there at twelve-fifteen. So sometime between ten o'clock when Woody saw her and twelve-fifteen, she was gone."

"It must be the flowers," I said. "I'll call the florist. There's only two in town."

"There was no wrapper around the flowers," Gideon said. "I checked. Mrs. Velvet didn't recognize the delivery girl."

Woody leaned back heavily in his chair. My mobile phone, lying on the kitchen counter, rang. I went into the kitchen to answer, disentangling it from the charging cable. I checked the caller ID. "What's up, Ozzy?"

"Listen, I, uh, had a bit of a problem last night, and I spent some time at the jail." He sounded sheepish and apologetic, not uncommon for Ozzy after a bender.

"Yeah, I heard. I talked to Jake this morning."

There was a pause. "Oh. He told you what Boyd said?"

"No, he said Boyd was drunk. Why? Did Wulfson say something to you?"

"He gave me an earful." Ozzy laughed softly. "Not much of it made sense, though. He said that he had saved your life. He kept saying *she* was coming after you. He said he convinced *her* that he'd hurt your store instead of you."

"What? Who?"

"That's just it. He never said." Ozzy sucked in a deep breath. "He said she was trying to intimidate him, but he wasn't scared of her. But he was. I could tell he was from the way he acted when he said it. You know how a coward acts when they're being bullied."

"Sure. He never said who it was he was talking about?"

Another pause. "I think it was his daughter. Louise."

"That's right. Somebody said she was back here." I calculated quickly. "She's seventeen or eighteen now, right?"

"Closer to twenty. Yeah. He said something like 'I told her she was to blame, and she decided to fix things.' Or something like that." Ozzy blew out a long sigh. "I was a bit hungover and maybe I didn't get it right. But he was sure scared."

"Well, Jake's on his way to see him so maybe Jake can get some sense out of him."

"I wanted you to know, Reddy. Boyd Wulfson is a mean son of a bitch and if he's scared of somebody, then that person must be even meaner. You be careful."

"Thanks, Ozzy." I lowered the phone and plugged it in again then returned to the dining room. "That was Ozzy. He was in the drunk tank last night with Wulfson." I summarized what I was told.

Gideon pulled a small spiral pad from his back pocket and started flipping through the pages. "Louise."

"That's his daughter," I said. "Remember? We talked about her. She was put into foster care or something when Wulfson went to prison."

Gideon raised his head slowly. "It had to be someone close to him, someone who could get close to the victims, someone no one would suspect. It had to be someone with some knowledge of medical practices in order to induce a heart attack." He shifted his attention to me. "Your new clerk. What's her name?"

"Barb Forester."

"Forester," he muttered, flipping through his notes. Then he raised his head, his eyes bleak. "It's her."

"Who?"

"Barb Forester. It's her. She's doing it."

"What?" I leaned back as though I could put distance between myself and what he was saying.

Gideon tapped his memo book. "She was farmed out into the foster system. She was adopted by the foster family and took their name. Louise Barbara Wulfson Forester."

The name fell into silence. I shook my head. "That's crazy. She just moved back here. She said—" I suddenly remembered. *I thought I'd go into nursing.*

"It has to be her," Woody said, his voice rough. "She took a job to get close to you. No one in town would know her. They were recluses out there on their property. She never came in for school. She was home-schooled and had nothing to do with anyone here."

I jumped up and went back to the kitchen, to my phone. I dialed the store with trembling fingers. "Reed, hi, it's me. Is Barb there?"

"No, she never came back from lunch." Another pause. "She left around ten-thirty to get some stuff we needed at the hardware store, but she hasn't come back. I closed up for a few minutes and grabbed a sandwich from the café."

"Thanks, Reed." I ended the call and came back to the dining room. "She's not there. She left in mid-morning to run errands and never came back." I dropped into my chair, my knees trembling. "What's going on?"

"Today's the day," Gideon said softly, like he was speaking his thoughts out loud. "It's the anniversary."

"No, the accident was on October 1," I said.

"The anniversary of her mother's death." He flipped through his notes. "The wife was in a coma and had a heart attack and died. Where did she die?"

"What?" Nothing was making sense. "It can't be Barb. She's a kid. A young woman. Why would she do it?"

"Revenge. Reparation for her mother's death." Gideon closed the notebook and tucked it back into his pocket. "You said she was home-schooled. She didn't have many outside influences. Who knows what her father told her after that accident?"

I remembered someone mentioning the possibility of some kind of abuse. It made a horrible, twisted sense, especially when I recalled how Boyd Wulfson had consistently denied any responsibility for his wife's death. I was certain he'd try to shift the blame to someone else and who better than an impressionable child?

"Where did she die?" Gideon demanded. "The mother. That's what's important to her."

Her. Barb. "The hospital? That's where her mother had her heart attack. She was on life support." Gideon was shaking his head. "What?" I demanded. "Why is that wrong?"

"If it was the hospital that killed her mother, she would have gone after the doctors or the nurses, not your grandmother. Where does she blame you in particular?"

"The store?" My eyes widened. "The accident site. That's the place where we were all together."

"We should tell Jake." Woody pulled out his mobile phone.

"No. There's iffy cell service out by Wulfson's place. Call the station and leave word for him there."

Gideon stood. "That's it. The accident site. Let's go. You drive. How can we approach it and not be seen? Is there a back way?"

"I'm not sure," I said, thinking furiously. "It depends on where she might be. I wonder if she was the one maintaining that memorial on the roadside. Remember? It was on that hill off the road." I rose along with Woody, who walked with us to the back door.

I paused in the kitchen to pick up my phone and my car keys, putting keys in my jeans pocket and my phone in the holder on the left side of my waistband.

"Give me my keys." Woody held out his hand. "I'll move my car. Where's your shotgun?"

Gideon stopped in his tracks. "Shotgun?"

"In the car. And I have Sally." I pulled my sweater to one side to show my S&W 9mm pistol attached to my waistband on the right side. "She's small but mighty."

Gideon shook his head. "Yeah, I'm starting to see that. Do you name each of your inanimate objects?"

"Most of 'em." I had a sudden vision of Bob, my battery-operated boyfriend tucked away in a drawer in my bedside table. My face got warm.

"Listen, boy." Woody put his hand on Gideon's arm. "You bring my girls back to me, you hear? Rosie and Reddy. I don't want either of 'em hurt." He stared fiercely into Gideon's face. "If I was ten years younger, I'd do it myself."

Gideon nodded once, quickly. "I won't let you down. And Woody?"

"What?"

"If you were ten years younger, I'd follow you. Stay near your phone and man the comms. Let me know if the chief checks in or if anything changes at the CF, if they get any word. We'll go and find out if my suspicions are right." Gideon followed me out the door.

I went into the garage and sank into Stu's driver's seat while Gideon hurried around to the passenger side. I raised the door with the remote while Woody backed out behind us. I shifted into reverse as soon as Gideon was seated, twisting on the seat to check behind me.

"Where's your shotgun?" he asked, his face inches from mine.

"In the hatch, under the flooring with the spare tire." I glanced at him, no longer sure what I felt. Anger? Hurt? I was exhausted as though the emotions of the last two hours had finally caught up to me. I was tired of being used, tired of being lied to, and tired of love.

Love? Where the hell did that word come from?

"I suppose you named your shotgun, too," Gideon said wryly.

"I suppose I did." I focused on my driving, getting the car onto the street. I waved to Woody then we followed him out of my neighborhood where he went left, and we went straight.

"Well?"

"Mossy. It's a Mossberg Youth Bantam." I concentrated on the traffic around us which had increased when we entered town.

"That's the right size for you."

"Hmm."

I drove on side streets to avoid the traffic lights on Main Street. We went in silence for a minute or two then he said, "It started out as a simple way to figure out who was behind this. It turned into a whole lot more."

"Yeah, a lot more lies," I snapped.

"I didn't lie when I told Woody that everything

changed once I met you."

My hands reflexively opened and closed on the steering wheel, which I had encased in a gaily patterned cloth overlay of peace symbols, gaudy flowers, and smiley faces. I was anything but peaceful now.

"How much of it was true?" I blurted.

"What do you mean?"

"The tech stuff, your partner in California, your grandfather and the big drug company. How much was true and how much were lies?"

He was quiet for a long time. We were on the highway heading out of town before he spoke. "None of it was lies. I was targeted by upper management because of my support. I do want to help Julie with her ideas for the merging of your businesses. I do want to maybe move here and be with you."

"Bullshit." I clung to the steering wheel, my hands trembling.

"It's not bullshit. It's the truth. I know you're afraid of letting anyone into your life. I know you're frightened about letting somebody love you. Maybe it won't be me. Maybe I've hurt you too much. Maybe I've fucked this up so badly that I'll never have your trust again. But believe me when I say this. You're a special woman and you're someone I want in my life. I want to be with you, I want to love you, and I want to grow old with you." He gave a shaky laugh. "If we survive the next hour, that is."

I couldn't answer. I wasn't sure what kind of answer I could form to such a declaration. I'd known the guy for a week and in the last two hours I found out that most of what I supposed about him was false.

Or was it? Had I created a fabric around the reality? Was that fabric disintegrating now? Okay, maybe he did come here with one purpose in mind, and he used me for that purpose. Did that cancel out anything that happened between us?

"I can't think about that now." I hated it, but my voice was as trembly as my hands. "I need to focus on what we're trying to do. If what you said is true, Barb Forester is a murderous madwoman, and she has my grandmother hostage."

I slowed the car so I could hazard a glance at him. "My grandmother is the most important thing right now. Everything else can be revisited once I know she's safe."

"I know."

I focused again on the road. We were coming to the intersection, the makeshift memorial on our left. "I'm going past the site another half-mile along the road," I said when we stopped. "There are logging tracks through here, some marked and some not. We'll go further west then cut into the south and pick up a track that goes east. It hasn't rained too hard lately so it should be passable."

I thought about it then added, "It should intersect the gravel road that leads to Wulfson's place. We'll come up to this intersection from the south, the same way he did when we had the accident. Who knows? Jake might be on that road if he's done at Wulfson's place. It's further south on the gravel road about six miles or so."

"You know the territory," Gideon said. "I trust you."

The words hung in the air between us. Trust.

"I trust you to watch my back," I muttered. "I don't know what to do in a situation like this." The car inched forward. I forced myself not to peer to the left and the road leading to Wulfson's freehold.

"We won't know until we get there what we've got. Stay calm and don't make any sudden moves that might spook her." I heard movement and saw him pull his gun from the holster at the small of his back.

I swallowed hard and kept driving. The rutted logging road was on my left, barely seen in the undergrowth. We were downhill from the intersection and hidden from sight.

I made a left turn. We entered the forest.

Chapter 13

We were immediately dunked into darkness. The pines overhead formed a complete canopy, blocking out the sunlight. My car lights automatically came on to compensate, showing us a rutted, bumping "road" that disappeared almost immediately ahead of us given the twisting hillside.

I slowed to a crawl lest I tear out something from Stu's underside. As it was, there were grating sounds coming beneath us and branches scraped the sides of the car. Our windows were alternately draped then clear of pine needles and leaves.

It was like going through a car wash with the dangling ribbon things that swiped over your car. This went on for a minute or two with me leaning forward to peer at the terrain ahead.

"Careful there," Gideon said, pointing to the left. "I think the road ends."

"That's our turn." I carefully maneuvered to the right then twisted the wheel to the left, narrowly avoiding a tip toward a ditch on the right that dropped off into oblivion.

We entered onto a marginally better lane, less rutted and wider with fewer trees. The loggers had been through this area several years earlier and replanting had been done. The saplings were taller than my car but not as dense as the previous track.

"It's right ahead." I stopped the car. The hilly gravel road in front of us led on the left to the highway we'd just exited and on the right to Wulfson's homestead and a few others on this lane.

"We need to go on foot from here. We'll have a clear view of the highway once we top that hill and we'll be able to see where the gravel road comes out. If she's anywhere near the highway, we should see her."

Gideon opened his car door and walked behind the car, opening the hatch. I met him there. "Do we need Mossy?" I asked.

"I'd rather have a gun than wish I had a gun."

I pointed to the small lever that hid the spare tire compartment. He pulled it up and got out the shotgun then I retrieved the 20-gague shells from the holder, held in the side webbing.

Gideon loaded the gun then broke it open to hang over his arm. "Lead on."

I pocketed the extra shells and set off. Straight ahead was the gravel road, which would be somewhat easy to walk on. But immediately on our left was a stand of trees and beyond them was the meadow where the decaying deer stands were located. If we could get across the meadow, then we'd have a clear sightline to the accident site through the trees lining the highway side of the meadow.

I went to the road and craned my neck to the right. Jake was there somewhere, presumably at the Wulfson homestead, around the bend in the lane. If we were right, he'd gone to confront Boyd while Louise presumably was hiding somewhere with Grandmother.

If we were right.

My car was almost hidden from view because of the

weeds and trees near it. Someone would have to be scanning for it to see it. I turned to the left and began to walk, Gideon beside me.

"How far?" he asked softly.

"Not far. Around that bend." I kept my eyes on the ground, avoiding ruts and dips that threatened to trip me. To my left I could see the beginning of the meadow through the trees.

I went a few more steps then gestured. "Let's go through the clearing. There are trees on the other side. We can see over the hill at the road."

The ditch here wasn't too steep. Gideon led the way, half-sliding and half stepping along the embankment. I followed, doing more sliding because of my shorter legs. The ground was damp underneath the trees and full of decaying leaves, which made the footing even more like a slippery carpet.

We crested the ditch, Gideon giving me a hand up. In a few more steps we approached the perimeter of trees bordering the meadow. He raised a hand then put his finger to his lips. I nodded to show I understood, even though I didn't.

Gideon carefully raised the shotgun, pulling the barrel together with an audible click. He inched forward in a half-crouch, ducking under the tree limbs that formed a protective perimeter to the meadow. I followed him but I was so intent on my footing that I ran into him before I even knew he'd stopped.

"What's wrong?"

Gideon shifted to the right. I straightened and that's when I saw Barb Forester. She was in the shadows, in the abandoned and ramshackle hut. Her clothing—dark brown pants and a pale blue sweater—acted like camo, making her blend with the blue sky and the darkness behind her. In front of her was my grandmother, sitting on what appeared to be a stump.

Barb had some kind of pistol, large and black, in her right hand. It was inches from Grandmother's fragile neck.

I gulped, taking an involuntary step back. Gideon grabbed my arm and prevented me from tipping over into the ditch. I managed to find my balance, but it was a near thing.

"What are you doing?" I moved forward, my eyes on my grandmother. "Leave her alone."

Grandmother smiled. "Don't worry, Rebeka. It's okay." She wore dark slacks and a knit top with a big grinning pumpkin. I'd given it to her for her birthday the year before. She appeared calm and unworried. Her legs were crossed at the ankle and her hands rested on her knees. It was like she was in the waiting room at the doctor's office, mildly curious and perfectly at ease.

"I've been waiting for you. I knew he'd figure it out." Barb jerked her chin at Gideon. "He's smarter than those hick town cops. They never guessed a thing. They drove right past here."

"Those hick town cops are interrogating your father right now," I shot back. Why was I defending Jake? Granted, the clearing was mostly hidden so he couldn't have seen them, but still…

Whatever. I shook that notion to one side.

"He doesn't know shit. They can talk to that asshole all they want, and he can't tell them a thing. I did it on my own." Barb sounded proud, confident. Her eyes moved to Gideon. "Put down the shotgun. Slow and easy."

Gideon did as she commanded, leaning over and setting the gun on the ground then straightening. "What do you want?" His voice was conversational and calm.

He's done this before. He's a cop. He knows about shit like this. The knowledge steadied me, and I was able to relax my tense shoulders, standing a bit taller. Oddly enough, instructions from a yoga instructor from years ago sprang to mind. *Be in this moment. Let go of past regrets and future worries. Be now.*

Focus, I reminded myself. Focus.

"I wanted to kill the people who ruined my mother. Then I want to die." Barb spoke simply, as though her words made complete sense. "I deserve to die. I'm a killer."

"I know." Gideon nodded. "All those people. You must have so much guilt on your conscience."

She tilted her head slightly and frowned. "Forget them," she said dismissively. "I killed my mother."

"Your father killed your mother," I said. "It was his drunkenness and his bad driving that caused the accident."

"That's not true." Barb shook her head adamantly, stubbornly. "My father was arguing with me and because of that, he lost control of the car." She said it in a mechanical, singsong voice. Repeating what she'd heard over and over again.

"You said she was ruined. I don't understand," I blurted. "Who ruined your mother?"

Barb wasn't listening to me. Her attention was fixed on Gideon. I used her distraction and inched closer. Grandmother saw me move and shook her head slightly.

I studied Barb, marveling that I hadn't seen that maniacal glint, that haunted, frightened expression. Was she such a good actress? Or was I so stupid I didn't see it?

"Get rid of your gun." Barb gestured to one side.

I started to reach to my side then stopped. She was staring at Gideon. "What gun?" he asked.

"You're armed. Get rid of it." Barb leaned closer to Grandmother. "I'll kill her then I'll kill her." Her gaze skittered to me. "I can do it before you can move."

I watched Gideon absorb this then he held up his left hand, sliding his right hand along his waist. He pulled out his weapon and lifted it aloft.

"On the ground. Gently." Barb gestured to the discarded shotgun.

He did as she demanded, leaning over to set the Glock near the shotgun. He wavered slightly when he straightened.

"I have a bad leg," he said, wincing and rubbing his right thigh.

Right thigh? The bullet wound was on his left thigh. I'd seen it myself, an ugly mass of puckered flesh. Gideon's left hand lowered, and one finger moved slightly, pointing away from him and toward the left side of the glade. I shifted my weight in that direction.

Barb's attention swung to me then she continued studying Gideon, having determined that I wasn't any kind of threat.

"How did you get involved?" she asked him. Barb was turned a bit toward Gideon, but her gun stayed pointed at Grandmother. At least her hand was steady. Her right hand held the gun, and her left hand was clamped on Grandmother's left shoulder, holding her in place.

"You killed my stepdaughter." Gideon was tense

and coiled like a spring, ready to jump. I prayed he wouldn't. Lord knew what Barb would do if he did.

He's a cop, I reminded myself. He knows about shit like this.

"What was she?" Barb asked.

"What?"

Barb sighed, the sort of sigh an impatient parent would use when a child refused to speak. "What was she? They butchered my mother like a deer and passed her around to strangers. Was she heart? Lungs? Which was your stepdaughter?"

I gaped at her. "Your mother was an organ donor."

"She was not!" Barb screamed this so loud I cringed, longing to cover my ears. Her hand clenched convulsively on Grandmother's shoulder, and she gasped in pain. Barb shook her slightly, my grandmother's frail body swaying. "She would never do that! She would never agree to being butchered!"

"But she signed—"

Gideon shook his head. "Logic won't work here. Don't try."

"Shut up! You shut your mouth." Barb glared at me then Gideon. "Well? What was she? Heart?"

"Kidney."

Barb narrowed her eyes. I could imagine her ticking through some checklist in her mind. "The young one. She fought."

Gideon's hands clenched. "How did you do it? You must have had access to the transplant records. How did you find them and track them down?" His left fist unclenched, and his finger moved again.

I moved to the left. He was trying to separate us. That made sense. Make it harder for her to target us. I lowered my head to show I understood.

"Quit moving." Barb glared at me.

"How did you do it?" Gideon inched slightly ahead.

"Stop moving." Barb shifted position, too. We were now set up like a triangle with me and Gideon at each end of one side, Barb and Grandmother at the point ahead of us. Behind them was the rickety shed where light shone through cracks and holes, making a halo effect around both of them.

Barb glowered at us. "I'm not kidding. I can kill them before you can do anything. She can tell you." Her chin jerked toward me. "I'm a certified firearms instructor. I took it as part of my training. Tell him."

"She's right. It was on her resume." I kept my hands ahead of me at waist height, palms pointing downward. My gun was near my elbow. I knew I couldn't shoot her. I'd only shot at targets, never at anything living. I was pretty certain I wouldn't be able to aim at another human being. But I might be able to provide an element of surprise if she saw it.

"Tell me how you did it," Gideon insisted. "It must have been difficult."

Barb smiled bitterly. "All I had to do was screw the right guy. There's a records management system at the hospital that listed everywhere my mother was butchered and used. Once I had the name, I had to do a bit of research to find the people and decide on the best way to get to them." She frowned. "The tissue stuff was hard. That took more work."

"Tissue?" I asked faintly.

"You know. Parts used for burns and stuff."

"How many were there?" Gideon asked. "Total?"

"Ten."

I gaped at her. "Ten?"

She nodded matter-of-factly. "I wanted to do each of them, but I can't. It's getting too dangerous. I knew somebody would put it together sooner or later. I guess it was sooner."

Good Lord. She sounded so calm, so factual about the fact that she stalked and murdered ten people. I felt like I'd fallen into a rabbit hole and woken up in some alien land.

"But how did you do it?" Gideon asked. "How did you fake the heart attacks?"

"Oh, that was easy. The heart has an electrical system that controls the rate of the heartbeat. You have to disrupt that. Unless a person has a defibrillator handy, they'll be dead within minutes. That's why it was important to get them alone. That's what was the hardest to manage." She sounded completely blasé about it as though mapping out someone's death was an everyday occurrence.

For her it was, I realized. This was a woman who had tipped so far over the edge of reason that she could plot and carry out the deaths of ten people, murdering multiple people at one time in order to make sure they died on the anniversary date. She had plotted my death and Grandmother's, but she hadn't carried it out yet.

Grandmother cleared her throat. She didn't acknowledge the gun so close to her head. She stared at me, her gaze direct. "Tell me, Barbara. Do you have any children?"

Barb flinched. I held my breath, watching her finger tighten on the trigger. "What?"

"I asked if you have any children."

"That's a dumb question. I suppose you'll try to play

on my feelings, tell me to think what it would be like if my child was in danger and other bullshit." Barb's face twisted with anger, a harsh parody of the solicitous store clerk who helped elderly patrons.

"Not at all," Grandmother replied. "I was hoping that the stupid in your family would die out with you."

Barb didn't register the insult for a long second. Then she pressed the gun more firmly against Grandmother's neck. "You bitch."

Grandmother shook her head. "You poor child. Raised on hatred and fear. What kind of lies did your father tell you?"

"Shut up."

Grandmother raised her eyes to meet mine. She was unafraid. Of course she was. She'd been facing death for years. In many ways, it was an old friend.

"Your father was a monster, and he created another monster," she said softly. "Thank God you didn't breed and create even more. I knew your mother. She was a sad woman. Frightened. Lonely."

"She loved my father," Barb spat. "She adored him."

"She was desperately afraid. I spoke to her on more than one occasion. She was afraid to make a break for freedom."

Barb's hand wavered. "You're the one who talked her into it. It's because of you she died."

"It wasn't only her," Gideon said. "People in town knew. They knew he was abusing you. They knew what he did."

Barb's attention swung to him, defusing her rage. "That's a lie. He treated us okay. He never hurt us."

"There's all kinds of hurt." I picked up the story, praying my lies sounded believable. "We heard the stories. People talked about the Wulfson family and how odd you were, out there alone. I heard the rumors." I sensed Gideon moving, barely seen in my peripheral vision.

"I heard, too," Grandmother murmured.

I shook my head sadly, trying to keep Barb's attention on me. "I'm friends with the police chief. He talked about it. The only time anybody saw your mother was when your father was around to make sure she didn't run away. Especially after the accident. People wondered about you."

"That's bullshit! It's a lie! My mother loved my father. And he loved us."

I shook my head. As I did, I glimpsed movement on my left, in the trees bordering the clearing. My car was over there somewhere and the road leading to Wulfson's place was behind me and to the left, winding away out of sight. I didn't dare glance in that direction. Barb's attention was riveted on me which was unnerving, but which also gave Gideon the leeway he needed to continue edging away from me.

"I suppose it was bullshit, that stuff you told me when you interviewed." Where did that come from? What an inane comment. "How you admired me for being a woman in a male-dominated field and that crap."

"I meant it. Maybe admire is too strong a word, but I respect what you did with your business." Barb stared at me. Her sweater rose and fell quickly. I could tell she was struggling to contain her rage. "Did she tell you?"

"What? Did who tell me what?"

"The woman in the store. That Rhea woman. Did she tell you she recognized me? I only saw her for a minute. I wondered if she recognized me."

"She said you were familiar." What strange turn had this conversation taken? I was like a yo-yo, bobbing around and trying to figure out up from down.

Barb snorted. "Yeah, she got a good look at me when I hit her with the car."

I took a step forward, my fingers flexing. "You? You hit her?"

"Of course. I needed to get close to you. A clerk job in your store was the right thing to do. She was supposed to die. I guess I didn't hit her right."

My mouth sagged open. "You targeted her? You hit her?"

Barb made a dismissive noise. "Quit being stupid."

"Stupid?" I was so angry I was shaking. "You almost killed her. You left her to die by the side of the road."

Grandmother's eyes moved to her left and widened. I started to follow her gaze then stopped myself. Barb saw it, though.

"I told you to stop moving!" She raised the gun away from Grandmother, aiming at Gideon, who had swung to my right, forcing Barb to turn to get him in her sights.

I had a chance. I managed to pull my gun and raised it, my arms trembling. I had only used it in training classes and on the target field three times a year. She was in my sights, but I couldn't do it. I couldn't pull the trigger.

Barb saw my hesitation from the corner of her eye. "I knew you didn't have it in you."

"Kill her!" A voice screamed from behind me.

I instinctively swung to face the threat. Boyd Wulfson was a few feet away, peering at us through the trees. His face was a rictus of anger. "Kill her!" he screamed again.

It happened fast. Was he yelling at me or Barb? My finger squeezed. A gunshot. Wulfson ducked. I whirled when I heard another gunshot. My God, was it Grandmother? Was she hit? I remembered enough from my firearms safety class to lower my weapon lest I shoot someone.

"Reddy? Are you here?" A voice was yelling from the road behind me.

Where was Gideon? Grandmother?

There. On the ground. Grandmother lay in the dirt in front of the stump. Barb was standing over her, the gun still in her hand. Where was—I whirled.

Gideon was on the ground, a small pistol in his hand. Where did he get a gun? The hem of his jeans was crinkled, and I saw a holster strapped to his ankle.

He's a cop, I thought dumbly. Of course. He had a backup.

I spun again and started to run to Grandmother. She raised her head. "No!"

I stopped so fast I over-balanced and fell to my knees, sprawling with my hands outstretched. That might have saved my life. Barb fired again but it missed me, the bullet digging into the ground inches from my splayed fingers. I reflexively curled into a tight ball as two more gunshots sounded.

An eerie silence hung over me. I cautiously raised my head.

Grandmother was nearby, lying on her side. "I'm okay," she said breathlessly. "I fell over when he shot her."

What? When who shot her? I pushed to my hands

and knees. Barb lay on her back, sightless eyes staring at the sky, her legs stretched into the old shed. The blue sweater was turning color, staining red.

I swung my head. Gideon lay on his back, his gun still raised. "Are you okay?" he called, sitting up.

"You killed my girl!" Wulfson crashed through the undergrowth on my left and descended on me, fists raised. "I'll get you for this, you bitch!"

His words stopped abruptly when I dropped back on my butt and raised my gun. "If you take one more step I'll shoot you, you son of a bitch."

"Reddy? Jager? What's going on?" Jake and a deputy came barreling into the clearing from the road, guns raised.

I lowered my gun. "I have no idea," I admitted, then I fell back.

****

"She came into my apartment and said she'd help me get a vase from the cupboard." Grandmother sounded calm and composed but her hands on top of her cane were trembling, making it quake. "I didn't know her, but I don't know all of the delivery people, so I thanked her and let her in."

Jake had taken over as soon as he entered the meadow. We were briskly searched, we surrendered our guns, then we were bundled into squad cars for rides back to town. A deputy drove my car behind us. When we got to the police station, Gideon, Grandmother and I were separated and interviewed in separate rooms. Then we were taken to a conference room.

Woody had been waiting for us at the police station. When Jake suggested he might want to wait in the lobby, Woody shot him an exasperated glare and put an arm around Grandmother's shoulders while leading her into the room. Gideon sat on the side opposite us while Jake and the other police people took seats at the ends of the oval table.

"Why did you go to the meadow?" Jake asked me, not for the first time.

"You were covering Wulfson's house. I figured the accident site might be pertinent." That sounded good, I thought. I didn't want to malign Jake's police instincts. "I knew we could see the site from the meadow. I didn't know Barb and Grandmother were there. I didn't know she was waiting for us." I swallowed hard, remembering the bloody mess that was Barb's chest, so obvious against the blue sweater.

"You went armed." Jake said it flatly, his gaze going from me to Gideon.

I started to speak, but Gideon said, "As I said before. It seemed prudent." He and Jake stared at each other for a long moment.

Jake cleared his throat. "Yeah. Prudent. You fired two shots."

"I did. The first one hit her shoulder and spun her. That allowed Mrs. Davis to drop to the ground."

"And I did," Grandmother said proudly. "I pretended to faint. That psycho bitch was so surprised she let go of me."

Jake, the police stenographer, and the other deputy in the room all blinked widely at my grandmother's casual profanity.

"Once I saw she was clear, I fired again. By then the suspect had turned and was aiming at Reddy. The suspect fired and almost hit her." Gideon watched me across the table that separated us. His pale blue eyes were sympathetic. "I had a clear shot, and I took it."

"Where did Wulfson come from?" I demanded. "Weren't you interrogating him?"

"We did. He said he had no idea about what happened to Mrs. Davis. I didn't believe him, so we parked on one of the side logging roads and waited. Sure enough, a few minutes later he went sprinting down the road. We followed him and saw him pushing through those trees near your car." Jake's gaze traveled from me, to Grandmother, then finally to Gideon. "You said she murdered ten people."

I heard the disbelief in his voice. "I heard it, Gideon heard it, and Grandmother heard it. She did it." I glared at him, daring him to doubt me.

Jake studied the sheaf of papers in front of him, shuffling through them. I think it was our statements. He stared at something for a long moment then he raised his head, his gaze taking in me then Gideon. "There'll be a formal investigation. You won't be allowed to carry a weapon until that's concluded."

"I hope I won't need a weapon," Gideon said mildly. "I do plan to return to California, but I can come back if I'm needed to give testimony."

I stilled, forcing myself not to gape at him. How the hell could he leave after this? Was it so pedestrian an event that he could walk away?

Then I knew, with a sinking feeling in my stomach, that he could. It had been a lie, all of it. He only wanted to find a killer. I was just a sideshow. I sighed.

"Make sure that we have your contact information in case we do need it." Jake turned to me. "You fired your weapon. Were you aiming at Wulfson?"

Gideon stiffened but I spoke before he could. "No, I

242

was startled. I squeezed the trigger without thinking about it." I narrowed my eyes and tapped a finger on the table. "That asshole can't pin an attempted assault charge on me. If he tries, I really will try to shoot him and this time I won't miss." I leaned back and crossed my arms. "That's my story and I'm sticking to it."

The stenographer grinned then ducked his head.

"We'll have written statements for you to review and sign." Jake pushed away from the table. "I'll make certain the regional FBI office has copies of everything."

"Thank you. Is that all?" Gideon stared around the table, challenging. I wondered how our small-town police department measured up in his experience. Or did it matter? Hell, he was leaving. What did he care?

"For now. If I have questions, I'll be in touch." Jake left the room, the deputy and stenographer trailing behind him.

"Now what?" I asked.

"Now you go on about your life." Woody helped Grandmother to her feet and enfolded her in his arms. "That was way too much excitement for me."

She rested her head on his shoulder. "I know what you mean. I think we need to go home, fix a drink, and relax."

He kissed her cheek. "Your wish is my command." Woody winked at me and led her away, their arms firmly interlocked.

I stood, wobbling a bit and followed them out. I sensed Gideon behind me. We walked through the station and came to the front door. Night had fallen while we were being interrogated. It was snowing, fat flakes sparkling in the streetlights.

I watched Woody escort Grandmother to his car

then he waved at me and got behind the steering wheel.

I turned. Gideon was watching me. "Your car is at my place," I said. "I'll give you a ride."

"Thanks."

We went down the steps to Stu. The windshield was already covered by a half-inch of flakes. I drove slowly through the quiet town streets. I didn't know what to say. How do you say goodbye to somebody who saved your life? How do you say goodbye to somebody…you might love? We were silent on the way to my driveway.

I drove Stu into the garage, and we got out. "You're going home soon?"

"Tomorrow. I have a late day flight."

"Good to get out before the snow flies." Then I raised a hand and let the fluffy snow melt on my palm. "Well, you know. If you don't go now, you may get snowed in. Once winter sets in, it can be a challenge to travel on these roads."

"I don't mind a challenge." He kept his eyes fixed on me. "What about you?"

"Hmm?"

He moved closer. "Are you ready for a challenge?"

What was he asking? I looked into his blue eyes. Trust? Lie? What had happened?

Yes, he had used us to get to the truth. But did that matter, really? It all boiled down to whether I could believe him or not. I wasn't sure, but I knew I wanted to find out. I also knew that if I didn't give him at least a chance I might regret it for the rest of my life.

These thoughts and more flew through my mind in the time it took to blink.

I nodded and blew out a long breath. "Sure. I'm ready."

****

March 21

I checked my phone. Where was he?

I was sitting in the San Francisco airport, waiting for Gideon to join me. We had alternated trips between the Left Coast and Perrault for the past few months with Julie and Reed managing the store in my absence.

Gideon spent January in Perrault, which proved to be a real test because we had a record snowfall. We had a few dogsled adventures that were a challenge, but he professed to love it, so I didn't question him. He handled the sled teams like a champ and even managed a respectable fire in the lodge fireplace when we stopped for the night.

He drew the line at winter camping, though. "I want a warm bed and a warm woman," he said when I suggested it. "And believe me, you may be warm but you're not warm enough to offset six inches of fresh snow."

I didn't argue.

Now we were off on the first day of spring for a two-week vacation to Hawaii. I checked my text messages again. Rhea sent me a photo of her and Reed at the store with Julie. They were settling in nicely as co-owners. Our business arrangement with Julie had worked out well.

Gideon slid into the seat next to me. It had only been a week since I'd seen him, but my heart still did that crazy two-step when he was near.

He held up a couple pieces of paper. "I upgraded us. First Class."

"Wow. Pricy."

"I can afford it. I got a full-price offer on my condo."

He smiled smugly.

I smiled inanely then his words soaked into my bemused brain. "You what?"

"I did what you said. I survived a winter. And I think I survived it pretty damn good. I know this is where I'm supposed to be." He frowned. "Well, not here, but with you. And I think you feel the same way."

He handed me one of the papers then he stood, got down on one knee in front of me, and raised a small box. "Will you marry me?"

"What?" I stared at the ring in the box then at his expectant gaze. "What?"

"Look at it." He flicked a finger against the papers I held.

I studied the paper. *Marriage license application.* "What?"

"We can get married in Hawaii. We'll fill it out on the flight. What do you say?"

I stared at the application form then at him then at the small ruby ring in the little box. Then I began to grin. "I'm ready," I said, leaning forward.

He met my lips in a long kiss. I vaguely heard applause around us then I drew back. Gideon took the ring from the box and slipped it on my finger. "Hang on."

He stood and went to a woman sitting across from us. She laughed and handed him a phone. "I had her video it. I need to send this to Woody."

Several strangers nearby shouted their congratulations. I laughed and wiggled my hand for everyone to admire my new jewelry. Then my phone blasted out "Tuxedo Junction." I answered the Facetime call.

"You can't change your name!" Grandmother

declared, smiling broadly.

Gideon held up the tickets and the application. "Ready?"

"Sure. I'm also ready. Whenever you are." I looped my arm through his and we headed for the plane.

A word about the author…

J L writes 'mystery with a touch of romance and romance with a touch of grey'. Join her on Facebook (https://www.facebook.com/jayeAtplay) or her website to stay in touch.

www.jayellwilson.com

www.ingramcontent.com/pod-product-compliance
Lightning Source LLC
Chambersburg PA
CBHW070105030726
47506CB00002B/605